Piano in the Dark

Piano in the Dark

Eric Pete

www.urbanbooks.net

Urban Books, LLC
78 East Industry Court
Deer Park, NY 11729

Piano in the Dark Copyright © 2011 Eric Pete

ISBN 13: 978-1-60162-240-2
ISBN 10: 1-60162-240-6

First Trade Paperback Printing January 2011
Printed in the United States of America

10 9 8 7 6 5 4 3 2 1

Distributed by Kensington Publishing Corp.
Submit Wholesale Orders to:
Kensington Publishing Corp.
C/O Penguin Group (USA) Inc.
Attention: Order Processing
405 Murray Hill Parkway
East Rutherford, NJ 07073-2316
Phone: 1-800-526-0275
Fax: 1-800-227-9604

Acknowledgments

Hey, everybody! We're now up to number ten and I look forward to sharing more novels with you in the future. With all your choices in today's market, I appreciate your picking up my newest. If this isn't your first novel by me, thanks for coming back. If this is your first time, I hope you go back and check out my other works such as *Someone's In the Kitchen, Lady Sings the Cruels, Blow Your Mind, Sticks and Stones, Reality Check, Crushed Ice*, and many more.

This story you hold has had its share of stops and starts for a variety of reasons. I guess I kept trying to wrap my mind around some of the core themes and concepts, letting them marinate until they were ready to be shared. I'd begin another story, but kept getting drawn back to this one as I tried to figure out would it work . . . *could it work*? Wondering what that means? What *it* is? You'll have to read to find out, my friends.

First off, I have to express my appreciation of the creative minds behind TV series such as *Lost* and *Fringe*. Thank you for challenging our notions, stimulating our imagination, and balancing that with the importance of the human condition. You inspire this humble writer.

I'm grateful for my family—Marsha, Chelsea, Mom, Dad, Virginia, and all the rest of my relatives and friends who've been there for me. An extra thanks to my bee-bee for reading those pages I set at your bedside in the middle of the night and for the honest feedback.

Acknowledgments

To Portia Cannon, thank you for wanting nothing but the best for me and my career . . . and for giving a damn.

To Carl, Martha, Brenda, Natalie, Maxine and the entire Urban family as well as Kensington: Thanks for walking with me on this journey and for all you do behind the scenes to get my books on the shelves.

Susan Farris, my subdural hemato-homie! Thank you for your valuable insight and answers to my medical questions once again. The discussions are always fascinating . . . and fun. You're a lifesaver in more ways than one.

To my ghost readers who somehow find the time, Jamie, Shontea, and Jacqueline. I know that as I write this you haven't had a chance to read *Piano in the Dark* (my fault), but can't wait for our discussions.

To the dude on the trumpet by North Oaks Shopping Center at the corner of Vets and FM1960, thank you for playing that day, sir. You never know which seeds may blossom.

To everybody that came out to the *Crushed Ice @ Crush* book premier, my first time doing such an event, thanks for making it magical. Special shout-out to Blake Boyd, Andrew Grala, and the rest of the Crush Wine Lounge folk. Always look forward to that next bottle of Riesling. Also have to thank Dianna Montoya of Karrelle Photography for the incredible shots and Michelle Hill of Borders for always vending with that smile. To all of my readers who made it out to my stops on the *Crushed Ice* tour, a hearty thank-you and big hug. ATL, I owe ya! Thanks to the booksellers who are always so pleasant as well. Special shout-out to the cities where I've hung my hat from childhood into adulthood—Seattle, Lake Charles, New Orleans, and Houston. Glad I got to hit all of you on the last tour. Seattle, thanks for making my homecoming so special. Promise not to make it so long before you see me again. West Seattle, kid!

Acknowledgments

Immense gratitude to the book clubs for welcoming me and my creations into your homes, your meetings and, most of all, your hearts. The discussions and hospitality I've experienced have been some of the highlights of my career.

Thanks to the reviewers and media who find the time for me and my works: Tee C. Royal and RAW-SISTAZ, Yasmin Coleman and APOOO, Adai Lamar of KJLH, Radiah Hubbert and Urban Reviews, Hal Clark of 98.5WYLD, Book Remarks, Joy Farrington, Kimberly Kaye of 96KIX FM, Thais Mills of LipServiceInk.com, Heather Covington of Disilgold.com and Literarydish.com, Nakea Murray, Erik Tee, Gina Cook and Big Boy Chill of 107JAMZ, Angela Jenkins of KBMS, Monica Pierre, Jackie Simien, Mista Madd and Brandy Garcia (GO NOLES!) of 97.9 the Box, Kandi Eastman of Majic 102.1, Ella Curry, Gail Norris, Nancy Parker-Boyd, Dionne "Diva" Character, Dedan Tolbert, Jake McDonald, LBJ and Kelder Summers of Old School 106.7, Tony Jones of the McLean County Urban League, and Glenn Townes.

Last, but far from least, to my fellow authors and friends who continue to dazzle the world with their literary skills and boundless imagination. Shout out to a few of 'em: Kimberla, Dwayne, Victoria, Kendra, Tracie, Marissa, Lisa, Mary, Victor, Lolita, Reshonda, Pat, Donna, Jessica, JL, Karen, Earl, Monica, Linda, Gloria, VeeJay, Lissa, Electa, Nancy, and Shelia. To all the up-and-coming authors, *don't stop believin'*! Yeah—a Journey reference. I went there. Sue me.

I'ma go 'head and wrap this up, so you can meet these new characters. They're waiting for you.

No. Really.

They're waiting for you.

If you want to keep up with moi, stop by <u>www.Eric-</u>

Acknowledgments

Pete.com and let me know how you're doing. Follow me on twitter: @IAmEricPete or join the ERIC PETE Readers group on Facebook. *Or* if you're really, really adventurous, you can me at 1-800- . . . *click* <*Dial tone*>

Can't stop. Won't stop. Believe that.
-E.

Now—Rayne, Louisiana

We stare each other down. Neither wanting to budge from our position. But I've come too far to back down. So many resources exhausted, including my patience as well as my soul.

"You sure you cain't wait 'til tomorruh?" he asks, pulling his slicker close to his grizzled face. His chewed-up cigar has long been extinguished, yet he doesn't relinquish his toothy grip. One hundred percent misery with a chance of despair is forecast for today. My arm, although fully healed, aches. My shoes are ruined by the deep, muddy puddles before I even travel a yard.

I consider his request, but don't relent. I have to know. "No. I need to do this now," I reply.

He grimaces before considering what I've paid him for this task. "Suit yourself," he says with a shrug. A crack of thunder erupts, announcing the next harsh downpour. My tiny umbrella from Walgreens has long succumbed to the brutal gusts, offering me nothing but the illusion of shelter. Rain's coming down so hard now that I have to focus just to see him as he restarts his hasty clip. Headstones and markers of bygone eras only serve as the briefest of obstacles to someone as familiar with the grounds as he.

I quickly pursue, wondering if after all the searching that I've finally come to the right place. And if he knows what he's talking about. My pulse is racing and part of me wants to puke. A raw mix of exhaustion and nerves. I swear if this is a wild goose chase, I'll kill him.

"Should be right about . . . here," he proclaims, trying to read from the hastily torn piece of paper removed inappropriately from the church records he'd spent days sifting through. I rush past him, eager to put the haunting to rest. Through the deluge, I read the words etched in the worn stone.

"This isn't it! This is not frickin' it!" I belt out. The surly old Cajun doesn't take kindly to my barking. Probably wants to cause me grave bodily harm.

"Wait, wait," he says, acknowledging my frustration before it boils over. I watch as he flips the paper in his hand, scowling as he deciphers it. "It's over there," he says, having righted his treasure map. He points at a different section of Saint Joseph's Cemetery, newer than where we are now. Makes sense. More puddles to navigate. I lower my ruined umbrella, considering whether to abandon it if not for hallowed ground.

"C'mon then!" I yell over the din, nature's fury telling me to leave well enough alone. I can be hardheaded. We continue our march through the graveyard, my own personal Trail of Tears, until he stops. A final glance at the barely legible scrap in his hand and he nods.

"Here," he solemnly says, the cigar fragment wiggling between his teeth. "Dis it here."

He steps aside, bowing his head as he makes the sign of the cross. I get down on one knee, muddy water soaking through my pants leg and chilling me further. I silently mouth the name on the headstone while reverently touching the tiny gravesite, my search at its end. I feel the lump welling up in my throat and try to suppress it. "I found you," I mumble, more out of astonishment than accomplishment.

"Loved one?" he asks, daring to interrupt the moment.

"You might say that," I answer, not taking my eyes off the grave that held a small child. Rainwater continues to run down my face with a steady stream rolling off my nose.

Who knows tomorrow's plans for you, I think to myself, those words having once been said to me by another.

1

I groaned as Bruce Springsteen's "Glory Days" reverberated through the midtown pub for the second time in a row, finding fleeting solace instead in the bottom of my empty shot glass.

"Tell me again why we came here on karaoke night?" I asked my boy Jacobi as I raised my hand to request another round of Cuervo from the attractive waitress. As before, she held her smile a little longer for me. Lips curling to which mine reciprocated.

"Because the drinks are cheap. Duh."

"Like you don't have enough billable hours to afford a private room at Downing Street."

"True enough," he agreed, never one to let something like humility get in his way. The only time Jacobi used the word *humble* was when he dropped the *H* sound and referred to the town of Humble north up the Eastex Freeway. "But the pickings here are better. Even if they sing like scalded cats."

"I'm not here for that, man," I reminded him before he tried to get me in some sort of trouble. "I'll leave the pussy-chasing to you."

"Whose fault is that, idiot? You were my role model in law school." The silent *now look at you* was almost palpable in the air, hovering like a big flashing neon sign over us whenever too many drinks were consumed. Especially when too many drinks were consumed.

Jacobi finished law school at TSU, Texas Southern University, while I simply unfinished . . . dropped out with a bunch of student loans and no shingle to show for it. Now I worked for Casey, Warner & Associates, the same law firm as him, but as his paralegal. But I was happy. Yeah. That's it.

"I'm happy with my decisions, man," I said, vocalizing my thoughts as if some sort of therapeutic exercise. "You wish you had a wife like mine."

Before he could string together a remark, my iPhone rang in my jacket pocket. Speak of the devil. Thinking back to our argument before I came out here, I decided to ignore it. Disagreements were the currency in which we exchanged these days. The sounds of frolicking and cavorting in the background during a phone conversation with Dawn would only make things worse. I'd deal with her and my impending hangover when I got home.

"Speak of the devil?" Jacobi joked, reading my mind as any close friend could. He was also the best man in my wedding.

"Yeah. Too noisy in here, though. I'll text her later."

Another round of shots was delivered to us. Jacobi thanked our waitress, slipping her an early tip along with his business card. The same waitress who'd shown definite interest in me all night. I started to say something to Jacobi, but declined. This was his game, not mine. I was here to put my problems on hold, not to generate new ones—no matter how attractive.

Jacobi smiled. Teeth as impeccable as his attire. "Like you said, man. You're happy with your decisions."

Several bad songs later, it was closing time. Pathetic as it was, we were carrying on like this on a weekday. Boys afraid to grow up. Jacobi offered me to sleep it off at his place, a luxury condo on Binz Street near Hermann Park and Rice University, as he had his designated driver chosen. I declined, watching our waitress for the night as she maneuvered his Range Rover from the curb and left me to my own devices with a honk of the horn and thoughts of how differently things could've gone down. A lot could've gone down differently. I could be that high-priced hotshot lawyer on the cover of all the right magazines in Houston. But that wasn't the choice for me.

I stood outside the pub on the ever quieting street, debating whether to head straight home or grab some coffee at a Waffle House and sober up first. Spring, to the north where I lived, was a haul in my current state.

I unlocked my Camry with the remote. Decided to rest against it and take in the sticky night air before driving off. The missed call from earlier still shown on my iPhone. In a typical instance of too little, too late on my part, I sent a text to Dawn.

Worked late on big case with J. Be home soon.

I was almost the sole refugee from closing time at this hour.

I took a few deep breaths, sampling the spent residue of a depleted midtown in an effort to clear my head. The intake reeked of big talk long over and alcohol-induced false promises. Soured by the atmosphere, I prepared to enter my car and leave.

Except I wasn't alone.

What was strange was that I knew before I'd even turned to look. An awareness I'd never experienced before.

A woman in a simple black dress stood near the corner of Bagby and Webster. Under the streetlights, she appeared almost ethereal in nature. Lonely. As if, for that moment, she were the captive subject in a French painting or something with the city as her backdrop. Long ebony hair obscured her face, making me more than mildly curious. Rather than crossing the street and getting on with her purpose in life or whatnot, she just . . . stood.

Stood kind of like the hairs on the back of my neck, telling me something was either very wrong or strangely right. The area was relatively safe for me at this time of night, but all that was needed was opportunity in the form of a lovely victim such as herself to make the headlines of the morning's *Chronicle*.

"Ma'am," I called out politely and in an as sober as possible fashion. "Are you waiting on a taxi or something? Because the bus isn't running for several hours and it's not safe for you."

"I'm fine," she said calmly. She was stone cold sober. "Thanks for your concern, but I'm okay. I live around here—"

I startled her. Had to come closer for some reason. Hit the remote to lock up the Camry again as I stepped back onto the sidewalk to join her. Was as if something was drawing me in despite my needing to be on my way. Something more sobering than Waffle House coffee.

"Didn't mean to scare you," I offered as my tired, red eyes adjusted to the streetlights. She was beautiful—a basic, but apt description of her. She was little paler than what I was accustomed to, but with smooth, flawless skin, the sister appeared almost East Indian. Tall in her heels, she looked to be about five foot five with them off. Beneath her full eyebrows, her piercing brown eyes glistened; eyes that seemed almost alien and exotic under the light. Okay. The tequila shots had taken their toll on me. "Just wanted to make sure nothing was . . . wrong."

As I spoke, those eyes of hers flared in recognition. It was as if a new energy manifested and suddenly erupted from her. It overcame me and rendered me speechless. "Oh my God. Chase," she said, her voice wavering.

It wasn't a guess or a question coming from an addled mind. She knew me. Somehow she knew me.

But I'd never seen her before in my life.

2

"Chase, is it you?" the stranger said, overcome with emotion for reasons unbeknownst to me. She came forward and embraced me in a hug stronger than which I would've thought her capable.

"Yes," I answered, feeling embarrassed at the moment. "*Do I know you?*"

She didn't answer at first, just clung to me. Left with no choice, I kind of enjoyed the moment. I smelled deeply of her hair as her head rested on my shoulder. The fresh coconut was pleasing to my nose. On instinct, I allowed my hands to touch her in return, lightly rubbing her back.

After another moment or so of our corner convergence, she let go and backed away. "I'm sorry about that," she said, almost giddy as she stared at me. What was up with that? Perhaps I was wrong about her being sober. "I hadn't seen you in . . . in a minute. It's just nice to see a familiar face out here."

"I'm sorry. Did we go to school together?" I asked, trying a different approach to cover for my poor recollection. Shame on me for not remembering someone who looked this fine.

"Yeah. Yeah," she answered, either embarrassed by her actions or my reaction to them. "We met in college."

"Oh. Before law school." My mind kicked into overdrive, trying to peel back the years to that time in my life, when I was faster and more reckless with my partners.

"You're a lawyer?"

"No . . . no. Didn't quite work out," I replied with a nervous chuckle. "I do work at a law firm, though. Casey, Warner and Associates." Now I was volunteering information freely to a woman I still couldn't remember. But why did I feel so at ease with her? It wasn't the tequila shots and couldn't be the pussy because I didn't remember ever getting it.

"But that's not your calling, is it?"

"Sure it is . . . I mean. I'm happy. Wait," I said, pausing from my stammering. *What is your name?*"

"Ava."

"Well, pleased to meet you . . . again, Ava."

She chuckled. "Likewise, Chase." There she went again. Way too comfortable with speaking my name. The way she said it spoke of lazy afternoons and intimate dinners. Maybe something the future held if our "reunion" were to continue. And if I were a foolish man.

My iPhone buzzed. A text.

Thought you were on your way. Traffic can't be that bad this time of night.

Dawn was still awake. My sobriety was complete. "My wife," I offered to Ava with an awkward wave of my hand and inept smile. "I . . . I gotta go."

She tried to mask the disappointment on her face, but it slipped through the cracks in her resolve. I could tell she had dozens of questions, but decided not to pursue them. "Good night," is what she settled for.

The farther away from Ava that I walked, the more difficult it felt. I ignored the odd feelings, picking up my pace until I was once again at my car door.

No longer a captive of that painting, she'd begun crossing the intersection diagonally toward her secret, sexy cave wherever she dwelled. As she shuffled along with shoulders slumped, I wondered what magical things took place . . . or *could* take place in her midst.

"Ava?" I called out.

"Yes, Chase?" she replied, standing in the middle of the empty street. She straightened her shoulders and moved her hair out her eyes.

"Back in the day, what kind of person do you remember me as?"

"You were wonderful. Beyond belief."

I smiled just as my iPhone buzzed again.

3

On the long drive back to Spring, I questioned what had just happened outside the pub. A nagging part of me wanted to remain back in midtown with the mysterious woman Ava. She intrigued me, made me feel appreciated, but I left without even as much as a phone number. Better that way, I suppose. Company like hers at such an hour could come with a price. A price beyond idle friendship. A price I was unwilling to pay, I reminded myself as I pulled into the driveway of my home. As I hit the garage door opener, I didn't see any lights on in the house. Maybe my stalling tactics had paid off.

"Are you through avoiding me?" Dawn asked as I entered from the garage, throwing my keys on the kitchen counter. Rather than sleeping as I'd hoped, she was up watching television. The living room lights were dimmed and an empty wineglass sat on the coffee table in front of her. An episode of *Mad Men* was on AMC, harkening back to a simpler era, yet featuring a wife equally frustrated as she. Except I wasn't Dawn's Don Draper. He was successful in spite of his moral failings, things seeming to bounce in his favor, even. Don't think he would've had a meltdown over a stupid bar exam. Of course, that exam would've been a firm commitment. A commitment to a direction I still was unsure about.

I'd never win challenging her. Not as long as I was Robin to Jacobi's Batman. I'd always be stupid and foolish for being so comfortable in my standing. Every cell in my body said to go to our bedroom, take a shower, then go to bed. The path of least resistance and a soft pillow. But I was known for making stupid decisions. Just ask Dawn.

Instead, I sat in the wingback chair to her left, keeping some distance. Any closer and I might run the risk of being smacked. I removed my jacket and cautiously inhaled, looking to detect the sweet reminder of coconut amidst the tequila. Dawn wore a red silk nightgown over her slight, yet curvy frame. Crimson highlighting the sights along the highway that was her body. Her loveliness might've been rewarding if I'd brought my ass home earlier. "Something on your mind?" I asked, too frustrated by our current state to totally appreciate the view.

"Yes," she replied. "Like why you've been hiding out behind that womanizer Jacobi rather than coming home." She took the remote, pausing the nattily-clad sixties womanizers on the screen in mid-quip. The stilled television lights bathed her exposed mocha skin in an eerie Technicolor-ish glow as she swiveled to face me.

"I told you already. We had work to do. Gotta pay the bills, y'know. And I don't feel like arguing, Dawn."

"And from the way you act, you'd think I live for arguing. I just want to talk with my husband, but can't if he keeps avoiding things."

"Would it help if I apologize?" I said as I sighed. "I just want to go to bed."

Dawn clenched her teeth, still determined in her gaze. "He's about to make partner, isn't he?"

"So. He deserves it. Jacobi's put in a lot of time and hard work at the firm."

"Hmph. On your shoulders," she stated, waving her hands in the air. "Is that why you were out celebrating with him tonight? I know what's going on when you don't answer the phone, Chase. Drinking and whatever else."

I stood up, ready for a shower more than ever. Like I said, I'd never win challenging her. "I have a long day ahead of me, babe," I mumbled. Despite this disagreement, I loved Dawn. As I walked by, I leaned over and gently kissed her on the cheek. "I love you, girl," I said in her ear. She reached up, placing her arm around my neck in a semi-hug.

"It should be you about to make partner, sweetheart. You know he's only successful because you cover up for his mistakes. Then he takes credit for all your hard work. Y'know . . . one of these days, he's going to stab you in the back."

"Stop. Jacobi's my friend, Dawn," was all I could offer in response. Our argument was over for the night, but as sure as the day is long, we'd revisit it. As long as things stayed the way they were. Dawn wanted me to go back and finish law school and pass the bar. Questioning a man's heart and the choices he made was always a sure way to generate conflict. You'd almost swear she was unfulfilled instead of me.

But Dawn wasn't the only one to question me tonight. And I wasn't thinking about Jacobi, either.

That woman had questioned my calling.

A stranger, as far as I was concerned.

4

That night, while I slept with Dawn, I dreamed of another. We were back again at the corner of Bagby and Webster. This time, I stopped Ava from leaving. Told her about my insane urges and that I had to have her despite my reservations. And she agreed, putting my hands in places on her other than her back, which I'd innocently rubbed earlier. Placing my desperate tongue in her willing mouth, we made love beneath the streetlights. Aware of what the other desired so bad. Aware anyone could be watching. Aware we could be arrested. Aware that we didn't care.

But how do you make love to someone you don't know?

I asked myself that when I awoke from the crazy fantasy and went to work. It was an irksome thought I couldn't shake while I sat at my downtown desk at Casey, Warner & Associates on the forty-first floor of the Wells Fargo Plaza. Fending off that as well as my awful hangover, I downed some more of my tall Starbucks, checking Harris County court records online for filing dates on a case.

"Incoming!" Jacobi yelled, scurrying into my office with a stack of files. His crisp white shirt was already showing wrinkles. He'd come in early. Waitress must've not held his attention last night.

"Damn, dude. Trying to make me spill my coffee?" I scolded, quickly putting my drink down and clearing a spot on my desk for his newest pile of work. People around here always wondered how Jacobi could keep his office so pristine. Easy. He shuttled all of his shit over here.

I did my very best, taking pride in my work, despite pulling beyond my fair share around here. Growing up, I saw how hard things were for my mom on her own and she took way more shit than I. In this economy, I was lucky to be here. A smile led to certainty. So I was determined to keep my smile.

"Sorry. I need you to check on some case law for *Andrews vs. Stratford Circle* and look over these filings for the Hinijosa case."

"Good morning to you too," I said drily. "I thought you wanted the docket control orders first thing."

Jacobi chuckled as he folded his arms. "Dawn was pissed at you, huh? I knew it. Shoulda returned her call last night, fool. Maybe you wouldn't be so crabby now."

"Wouldn't have mattered . . . much," I said as I pinched between my eyebrows to alleviate some of the pain I was experiencing. "How in the fuck are you so awake? I at least went to bed."

"Took a Five-hour Energy," Jacobi replied. "Kicked the girl from the pub out, went for a three-mile run around the Rice University campus, then came in to work."

I shook my head. As with Dawn, sometimes there was no winning with my friend, either. "So, you want me to jump on this instead?" I asked, turning back to the new work he'd delivered as I heard Dawn's voice inside my head ridiculing me.

"Yes, please," he said as he prepared to leave me to my work again. "And I'm sorry for keeping you out last night, bro. Need me to talk to Dawn for you?"

Remembering her words about Jacobi, I replied, "Nah. I got it."

"You sure?"

"Yeah."

"We one hundred?"

"Yeah," I said with a chuckle of my own. I gave him an imaginary fist bump across the room. "We one hundred."

He'd almost completed his dart into the hallway when I did something against my better instincts once again.

"Jay?" I called out.

"Yeah?" he responded, his head extending into view in my doorway.

"Did you see this girl in a black dress at the pub last night?"

"I need more details than that, bro," Jacobi said as he fully backed up into view. "How'd she look?"

"Light-skinned sister with long black hair. Kinda East Indian looking. Beautiful."

"Oh. Damn. Probably one of them Louisiana redbones—Thibodeaux, Fontenot, Arceneaux, Bilbo?" he clowned, rattling off the last names in rapid succession.

I laughed. "Yeah, I guess."

"Nope. Definitely didn't see that last night, but wish I had," he said with a smirk. "Sounds a little like Lila Reed. Remember her? She used to be an attorney here. Think she moved back to Dallas to take care of her parents or something. Now *that* was a woman I would do in a millisecond."

"Probably as long as you'd last. A millisecond."

"I won't dignify that poor joke. Did you?"

"Did I what?"

"C'mon. Don't play any stupider than you are. You were a zombie a moment ago; now you're smiling like a rich kid with his first trust-fund payment. Did you get it? Did you chop it down? Did you wax that ass? My boy! I knew you still had it in ya!"

"Nah. Nothing like that, man. Happily married and out the game," I said, ignoring the dream still playing through my head on a continuous loop. A framed picture of me and Dawn in Italy on our honeymoon rested off to the left of a mountain of papers. We were standing outside the ruins of the Coliseum. "Just ran into her after you left. Innocent conversation. Says we went to school together, but I don't remember her. I can be bad with names, but never faces."

"Uh-huh," Jacobi said, eyeing me suspiciously. "Maybe she's had some kind of extreme makeover since you last saw her. Ugly duckling into a swan or something. I knew a few like that from back in my day. Girl was probably in your biology class, panties all wet and swooning, and you didn't even notice."

"Y'know . . . I didn't think about that. That's probably it."

"Glad I could solve your problem, bro. Now you know I can talk about fine-ass women all day, but can you please get back to work?"

"I'm on it," I said, smiling.

I got into my groove, working through lunch as I immersed myself in my work without any further interruptions from Jacobi.

My desk phone buzzed. So much for being interruption-free.

"Chase, are you there?" our receptionist Kelli Jo called out over the intercom.

"Yes. Somebody delivered something?"

"You got it, honey," she replied, her distinct east Texas drawl resonating through the speaker.

Most deliveries by courier to the firm that were for Jacobi and a few other attorneys were dropped off in my name for handling. Pushing away from my desk, I adjusted my tie and walked to the front.

Entering our newly renovated waiting area, I walked across the granite floors to the large mahogany receptionist desk where Kelli Jo was seated. Looking over her shoulder, the elderly guardian to our firm smiled at me as I approached.

"Good afternoon, sunshine," she gushed. "Working through lunch again?"

"Either that or coming in over the weekend, which the missus wouldn't like." I looked at the bin beside her. A single thin package rested there. "Is that it?" I asked.

"That's it, honey," she replied as she retrieved the package for me. "They weren't sure you worked here at first. Had to ask."

"Oh," I responded as I took it from Kelli Jo's hand. The package was clearly addressed to me, not to the firm or one of the attorneys here. There was no return address, which piqued my curiosity, but I still waited to get back to the confines of my office before opening it.

I peeled back the crisply folded taped covering to reveal a rush of vibrant colors. I carefully removed the contents, which turned out to be a tiny, framed oil painting: An abstract painting of what appeared to a lone man sitting at a piano.

I stared at it for a moment. Silent. Dealing with the unusual emotions evoked by it that contorted my insides. If you asked me, I'd be unable to put words to what I was feeling.

"Damn," I finally muttered as whatever had overcome me subsided. Maybe it was a gift from one of our business partners as they were known to do. Definitely out of the box on their part, but who sent it? I stuck my hand back inside the wrapping to fish for a note, a business card, or something. Nothing this unique could be anonymous.

I found nothing inside the wrapping, but almost missed

the tiny scrap of paper that had fallen onto my desk when I pulled the gift free. I held it up, reading the woman's handwriting.

> *Chase,*
> *So glad our paths crossed again. Couldn't get you out my head when I went home, so I worked on this. Hope you don't mind and hope to see you around in the future.*
>
> *-Ava*

I guess I wasn't alone in my dreams.

5

"What are you doing?" I asked into the phone as the remote arm in front of my car rose. I eased into the early evening light of the downtown street. A homeless man outside our parking garage waved a sign: *Spare change or a new Harley-Davidson. Either will do.*

"Well, I just picked myself up off the floor," my wife answered.

"Huh?" I said as I motioned the man over, offering up the change in my pocket and giving a thumbs-up to the humor of his sign.

"I'm in shock that you'd call this early, Chase. It's not even eight o'clock yet."

"Cute," I said, figuring out Dawn's jab at my recent activities. "No late night for me, honey. Wanted to see how you feel about dinner."

"Are you suggesting a dinner date? On a weeknight?" she teased.

Before entering the street traffic, I looked at my gift on the passenger seat, that kind artistic gesture from a stranger. "Yes. I'm suggesting a date," I replied with a chuckle. "Be ready. I'll call you when I get on the Hardy Toll Road."

"I love you," my wife said as I prepared to hang up.

"I love you too."

This was my attempt at mending things with Dawn. But midtown wasn't far from the office. *Only a diversion of a few minutes,* I told myself. That reasoning led me to

take a circuitous route home; a path that led me down
Louisiana under I-45 before winding my way over to Bagby Street. Couldn't hurt to see if Ava happened to be out
and about in her neighborhood. And all I wanted to do
was thank her for the thoughtful gift.

See her and be on my way.

Nothing to feel guilty about.

Yeah. Right.

I felt the same sensation, like last night. Little nee-
dles pricking my skin all over. Like the only way I could
eliminate this feeling was by pressing on. Crazy to think
odds would favor my crossing her path this easily, but
logic didn't have a place at the dinner table just now.

I slowed down as I came upon the pub again. Was Ava
a regular? Did she usually arrive early? Or was she nor-
mally one to shut the place down? Was she with anyone
last night? None of my business, but I wanted to know
nonetheless.

When I didn't recognize her from the people entering, I made a left turn onto Webster. It would give me
time to figure out whether I wanted to make another
round past the place or simply make my way home.
Just then, my iPhone rang out from its place in the passenger seat next to Ava's gift. I hadn't had a chance to
slap my Bluetooth on, so I reached over in case it was
Dawn calling. In spite of this minor detour, I wasn't
avoiding her tonight. Things were in a good place at
the moment.

"Hello?" I answered, preparing to say why I wasn't on
the Hardy Toll Road just yet.

"You're gone already?" my friend and boss Jacobi
asked. No doubt having stuck his head into my office,
he knew the answer, but his tone was more a plea that I
change my mind. I was his safety net at the firm.

"Yeah. Dinner with Dawn tonight. I got reservations

at Perry's Steakhouse for us," I stated so as to stop him from begging that I return to the office—an uncomfortable position I found myself in by virtue of not finishing law school.

To my right on Webster Street, several midtowners moved about on the sidewalk. Some were briskly jogging while others went about their business in a more leisurely manner—walking their dogs or strolling with their children before dark. Life in this trendy yet accessible section of Houston, where the expense of living near downtown was more annoyance than obstacle, was usually interesting to observe. I didn't hear anything else spoken by Jacobi at the moment as I singled out a lone individual from the rest. She held a full-sized brown paper sack and was walking toward me. Her long black hair bounced with each step. The buzzing jitters that had guided me here ceased.

Although the Randalls grocery bag only afforded me a partial view, I knew it was Ava. She couldn't have recognized my car from our short encounter last night, so I honked to get her attention. She was slow to react, looking in the wrong direction from behind her bag at first, before continuing her stride.

I was about to honk again, not seeing anywhere to pull over on the shoulder, when our eyes met. It was her. No doubt about it. She smiled, lowering the grocery bag from its high grip. I waved and broke into an equally generous smile. "I'll call you back," I said to a still-talking Jacobi just as I hung up.

As I dropped my phone back on the seat, I looked again toward Ava, expecting to see that same warmth emanating from her as before.

Instead I was met with terror as I rolled closer. The grocery bag she held fell, plummeting in freefall onto the pavement, its contents spilling out in disarray. I was thoroughly confused, unable to make out the words she was screaming in my direction. If I'd had more attention on the road, I would've understood immediately.

A dog.

A tiny Yorkie.

Amazing what one locks in on in times of stress.

It escaped its owner's control and had darted out directly in front of my car.

"Shit!" I yelled to no one but myself as I mashed down on the brake pedal, my foot threatening to burst through the floorboard à la Fred Flintstone. My Camry screeched to a halt, inertia sending me lurching forward until stopped by the firm tug of the seat belt. Everyone that witnessed it was as startled as the dog's owner, seeing the tiny dog scurry off to safety. I allowed myself a moment to retrieve my heart from my throat, knowing I'd prevented a splat on the street.

But when I turned toward Ava again, her face didn't share my relief. I only had a nanosecond to contemplate this before the world erupted around me in a flurry of thunder and broken glass. My head slammed back into my headrest as my phone and Ava's gift went sailing into the air, cast aloft by the violent collision I was enduring. As air bags deployed around me in this maelstrom, I was suddenly cast into blackness.

6

"Ow," I allowed to escape my lips when I finally dared move.

The woman standing by my bedside chuckled, rubbing my forearm in a comforting manner. She wore a lavender sleeveless shirt and a pair of tight-fitting jeans. "How do you feel?" she asked. Ignoring the question, I allowed my surroundings to register. The bedrails and smell of antiseptic were a sure giveaway.

A hospital room.

"Where am I?" I asked.

"Memorial Hermann," she answered. "Want me to get the nurse or something?"

"No. I'll live," I said as I strained to sit up in the bed. My neck was stiff and my face was sore, but fortunately it was milder than my last hangover. "What are you doing here?"

"I rode with you in the ambulance," Ava answered. "You don't remember?"

"No," I said, shrugging my shoulders. "But thank you for doing that."

"Do you know who I am?" she asked, her brow furrowing.

"Yes. I don't have amnesia. And I still know you about as well as I did last night, Ava," I joked. "How's my car?"

"Um . . . pretty bad. It was towed away. That big dump truck didn't see you stop for the dog and creamed you." Her eyes widened as she probably relived the moment.

"Oh. Got it," I said with a smile that didn't match the

state of things. In spite of my pain, it was comforting that she was here. But I had to be careful not to confuse her kindness with something else. "Why'd they let you ride in the ambulance anyway?"

"You want the truth?"

"Yeah."

I watched her redden with embarrassment. "Uh . . . I told them I was your wife," she said, turning away as her voice diminished.

"Heh," I chuckled. "You must've been bored to do that."

"No. Just wanted to make sure you were all right. I feel bad because I distracted you."

"Don't. It was my fault. Was looking for you anyway. To thank you for the gift. It's a very lovely painting. Unique. I like that."

"You're welcome," Ava responded, taking a mock bow. "I hope you didn't mind my going by your office to drop it off. I had no other way of getting in contact with you and last night, you said where you work."

"I did, didn't I? Sometimes I talk too much."

"It was always one of your adorable qualities, Chase," Ava said. It was as if she were looking not at me, but through me. And it wasn't just the meds they'd given me. Eerie. "Any other faults I should know about . . . since school?" she teased.

"My wife would say I have a bunch," I said with a grin. Then things really hit me as I looked at the clock on the wall, realizing the time. "Oh God."

"What? Are you in pain?" she asked as she touched me on my shoulder.

"No. My wife. I have to call her. She's . . . she was waiting on me. We were supposed to go to dinner. Shit," I uttered as I ran my hands over my face in frustration.

"She'll understand," Ava said as she reached in the back

pocket of her jeans and pulled out my iPhone. "Here. I removed a few of your personal items from your car. Didn't want someone stealing your stuff from the wreck."

"Damn. You're a regular guardian angel, aren't you?"

"I do what I can," she replied, sharing a smile with me quite like the one just before Scruffy's misadventure occurred. I didn't understand our connection, but it was there. This could've had a whacko stalker vibe, but it didn't.

Ava was about to say something just before I called Dawn, but the doctor interrupted both of us with a quick tap on the room door.

"How are you feeling, Mr. Hidalgo?" he asked, quickly reviewing my chart in his hand.

"A little sore, but ready to get out of here," I replied to the diminutive man in the lab coat.

"Well, it shouldn't be too much longer, sir. Looks like we're going to have some soreness over the next couple of days." Love how he said *we* as if he felt my pain.

He shined a light in both my eyes, then instructed me to follow it, speaking to Ava as I complied. "Mrs. Hidalgo, your husband has a mild concussion," he said, startling me momentarily. "He'll be okay, but I'm going to need you to continue to monitor him once he's released. Just be on the lookout every hour or so for any irregularities."

Ava didn't tell him any better, simply nodding in agreement as I curiously eyed her. She cut a mischievous grin my way. Absent her shopping bag, I had a chance to take her in fully minus the haze of a streetlight or drunken stupor. I could tell the way I looked at her made her nervous, yet also pleased her.

"That was good to know, wife of mine. Be sure to follow those orders," I teased as the doctor left us alone. Before joking any further, I told Ava to hold a moment as I returned one of several missed calls from my real spouse. Dawn must've been worried shitless when I didn't come home.

"Baby, it's me."

"Chase!" Dawn screamed loud enough for even Ava to hear. "What happened? Are you okay?"

"Yeah. I'm fine. Sorry about dinner. I was in a car wreck."

"I know," she said, out of breath as she scrambled somewhere. I heard a car door slam. Sounded like an echo wherever she was.

"You do?"

"It was on the news. It looked like your car and when you didn't answer your phone, I called Jacobi. He came get me. We just arrived at the hospital, baby."

"So you're not mad at me?" I joked.

"No baby. Not this time," she said with a nervous sigh. "See you soon."

I hung up, looking at Ava. "She's here," I said.

"I guess I better go then. Only room for one wife," she said as she leaned over, kissing me without hesitation. I didn't know how to react, but smelled the coconut again, taking me to my fantasy. She took her thumb and carefully eliminated any traces of lip gloss from my dry, tired lips. It seemed she wanted to tell me something else, but refrained.

"Ava," I called out as she walked away.

"Hmm?"

"I still don't really remember you, but I'm glad we met again . . . in spite of my car."

"Me too," she whispered as if hiding a secret from the world. "See you around, Chase. Get better."

I opened my mouth to call out, still at square one without a phone number or anything. When a female silhouette appeared in my door, I thought I might have another chance. But it was my beautiful wife instead, wearing the dress she'd probably selected for dinner, followed by a flustered Jacobi.

"Bro, what happened?" Jacobi asked, his lawyerly mind wanting to assess liability right away.

"A dog ran out," I said shaking my head as I avoided eye contact with my friend. "And I slammed on my brakes. I was just . . . stupid." He had to know roughly where the accident occurred, yet said nothing of it or what I was doing around there.

"We're just glad you're alive," Dawn said as she sat on my bed and embraced me.

"I'm not going anywhere, baby," I said as I held her tight. Dinner plans ruined because of me.

In addition to my phone, which Ava retrieved for me, a tiny framed painting rested on the table beside my bed. When asked about it, I told Dawn it must've been left by the hospital staff.

Concussion and all.

7

My alarm went off before daylight, bringing me out of my deep slumber. The standard call to arms at the beginning of my day. As I labored to move, I was greeted by stiffened parts beyond the usual morning wood. Felt like I'd been used as a punching bag for Floyd Mayweather Jr.

"Hey. What are you doing?" Dawn mumbled as she felt the bed shifting with my sitting up.

"Time to get up," I replied as I yawned.

"Uh-uh. You have amnesia or something? No work for you today. Go back to bed," she said as she rolled over in the direction of my voice. I watched her eyes softly open. Same enchanting eyes that greeted me for the first time back at Sam Houston State. Before my attempt at law school.

"You're my doctor now?" I asked of my once-upon-a-time math tutor.

"Nope. Just your nurse."

I didn't protest much when she nudged me back onto my pillow. In addition to her college-prep business, Dawn worked part-time at Macy's in the Woodlands Mall, but didn't go in until this evening. No dinner last night, but maybe we could work on dessert as she slid closer, her hand exploring beneath the covers.

"Sore?" she asked as her hand moved sensuously back and forth across my chest.

"Some. The muscle relaxers helped."

"Not *too* relaxed, huh?" she asked, her hand snaking past my waist.

"Um . . . you might be on to something there," I said with a grin as she awakened my dick with her skillful touch. I let out a deep sigh of relief, my remaining tension subsiding as Dawn pulled the covers off. She took me in her mouth, quickly coaxing me to a hard, effective state within the warm, inviting space beyond her lips. As she worked me over, I reached toward the curvaceous ass presented before me. I eased my thumb against her clit while probing the perimeter of her anus with my middle finger. Her asshole puckered at my touch, urging me to continue as she bumped her ass against my hand.

"Mmm-hmm," she mumbled, her mouth full of me, sending good vibrations through my body of the most wonderful kind.

In the bedroom, we never truly had problems. Problems existed whenever I put on my suit and ventured out beyond the bedroom walls. Where expectations were never met in someone's eyes. Maybe I'd stay here all day.

Dawn made that familiar sexy pop of her lips as she released her oral grip on my dick. She wiped the product of her labor from the corner of her mouth, then slid her nightgown over her head. I paused from kicking my underwear off my ankles to admire her.

I went to reach for her. To take her in my arms and kiss her like my life depended on it.

"Uh-uh. Take it easy," she said as she forced me onto my back. "Nothing too strenuous for you, big boy. Just lie down and enjoy."

I eagerly obeyed my nurse's instructions as Dawn mounted my erection, her hips quivering and flaring. I grunted as she lowered herself onto me, deliciously damp and wanting more.

True to her word, Dawn did all the work. After a shower, she found comfort in a peaceful sleep. Good for her, as I wasn't ready for a nap after all the activity of yesterday. As much as she'd object, I needed a moment to clear my head. I threw on some clothes and ventured out in her car.

Despite its tiny interior testing my current condition, I jetted down the street FM 1960 in Dawn's MINI Cooper to pick up a treat I knew she'd like. As the satellite radio played uninterrupted jazz on the Watercolors channel, I noticed the time. Close to noon. Rather than going to the Smoothie King at the corner of Red Oak by Houston Northwest Hospital, I proceeded the four extra miles to the next location by Veterans Memorial Highway.

Did one make better smoothies than the others? Probably not.

I was in front of the HB Japanese Steakhouse when my iPhone rang. I grimaced, suspecting Dawn had realized I was no longer in the bed beside her. Worse. It was Jacobi.

"What's up, bro?"

"Hey, Jay," I replied, lowering the volume to Paul Hardcastle as I placed my Bluetooth in my ear.

"Thought you'd be asleep. How you feeling?'

"Sore, but I'll live. Thanks for bringing Dawn by the hospital."

"No problem, sir. She's nursing you back to health?"

Thinking of our morning interlude, I chuckled. "She's taking care of me," I replied.

"Maybe get your mind off your old classmate."

"She's not on my mind, man. You saw I was taking Dawn out to dinner last night."

"Uh-huh. But where were you when you got crunched? Nowhere near your house. Don't think I didn't notice that."

"I'm not dignifying that with an answer. I was on my way home."

"Okay. You're lucky I'm not deposing you, though."

"I've seen you in action. Remember? You ain't so scary, bro. But debating your skills isn't healthy for my recovery. What's up?"

"Gayle's filling in for you and can't find the discovery responses to the Polk case in your office."

"That's because I left them in your office. It's the last thing I did before I left yesterday. They're on your desk beside yesterday's mail and your billing sheets for the month."

I listened as Jacobi fumbled around at his desk before everything went silent. "Okay. Got it, man. Thanks," he said. If he didn't call me from the courthouse later, I'd be lucky.

"Can I go now, boss?" I asked as I crossed Veterans Memorial, preparing to make a left turn into the Smoothie King parking lot.

"Yeah, bro. Sorry about calling you over this mess."

"S'okay. It's what you pay me for."

"Need anything? You car okay? Need a ride or something?"

"No. Dawn filed the claim with State Farm last night. Waiting to hear from them. I'll get a rental later today. Just trying to take it easy right now."

"All right," Jacobi responded, his voice easing. "I'll leave you alone, man. See you soon."

"Later, bro."

I ordered Dawn's Passion Passport and my Power Punch Plus. As I waited for my frequent customer punch card and the smoothies in the drive-through lane, I eyed an elderly man on the curb. Dressed in a pair of wrinkled khakis, flip-flops, dark blue socks, and a dark blue Hawaiian shirt, he sat comfortably on an overturned shopping cart with his back to me. It was a makeshift stage for a lunchtime performance.

I lowered my window some more, better to catch the notes from the trumpet he prepared to play. As the drive-through window opened, the employee handed me my card and the drinks along with my receipt. The man on the shopping cart blew.

The beginnings of "The Girl from Ipanema." He always warmed up with that song. Every time I watched him without his knowing. Call it nagging concern, but I'd been doing it more frequently these days. Having loosened up enough, his worn and weathered fingers were ready to perform admirably for the public.

I pulled away from the drive-through window, anticipating surprising Dawn with her favorite. But before I'd gone five feet, I stopped. Leaving the MINI Cooper running, I walked over from the drive-through lane and came over. He glanced over his shoulder, surprised to see me. He looked at least ten years older than what he really was. Despite that, we shared the same light brown eyes and skin hue. Without registering anything on my scratched face, I dropped a five-dollar bill in the white plastic bucket at his feet.

"Thank you, sir," he said with a nod and smile as he paused from his joy. I turned without speaking, returning to Dawn's car before someone thought about jacking it.

"How's your momma?" Joell Hidalgo, my father, asked after a single hastily ended note.

"Same as always," I replied loud enough for him to hear before I drove off.

Back to my world and away from his.

8

"Counselor, you know the court's rules about cell phones. I suggest you silence it while I'm in a good mood," Judge Akers offered from the bench. Her eyes beneath her excessive plume of red hair were exaggerated by her large, thick-rimmed eyeglasses.

"Your Honor, it's not mine," Jim Warner, one of the firm's distinguished senior partners, said as he looked inside the coat pocket of his suit. I was oblivious to the matter, trying to organize the documents I'd delivered for the large class-action case Jim was trying today. Until I realized they were both looking at me.

It was my phone. I'd forgotten to turn off upon entering the courtroom. Credit my returning to work a day earlier than what was prescribed by my doctor for the slip-up. My mind was still not fully back in gear, but I was needed.

"Sorry," I mouthed silently as I hastily ended the ringing. As it powered down, I had a moment to glance at the number of the incoming call. Not familiar. Probably a wrong number getting me in all kinds of trouble.

"Do you need to take that?" Jim asked as I went back to my arrangement of his presentation items and exhibits.

"No," I answered discreetly. "Probably a wrong number. I'll check on it later."

Later came during a recess to allow a key witness for our case time to arrive from the airport. It was an unseasonably warm and humid day, but I welcomed the chance to defrost outside along with the casts of potential jurors grateful for an escape from the frigid confines of the Harris County Civil Courthouse. Confidently clear of Judge Akers's edict, I retrieved my phone and turned it on as I leaned against the brick retaining wall.

"Hey, baby. Have a brief break, so figured I'd call," I said

"How are you feeling?" Dawn asked. Our agreement was that she let me go in to work and I would call at my first available moment.

"Good. Real good. I'm pacing myself just like I promised. Despite enjoying your company, I was going stir-crazy."

"Yeah. You were driving me a little crazy too with all your pacing. Couldn't even enjoy *The View* without you wanting to change it to CNN," she joked.

"Well, enjoy your TV, babe. It's all yours once again. I'm about to go back inside the courthouse."

"Okay. No working late, though."

"I promise."

As I prepared to shut my phone off once again, it buzzed with the delivery of a text message.

The message was a number I didn't recognize. Probably same as my earlier missed call.

How r u feeling? It read.

Better. Thx. Who is this?

I rapidly replied as I looked at my watch.

Are you alone?

Kinda.

I texted back, wondering who could be toying with me like this.

Jacobi, stop playing. U know I'm in court.

I sent upon further thought.

Wrong guess. Now my feelings r hurt.

Oops. Sorry. L I gotta go. Who is this?

Gotta w8 now since u guessed wrong. I'll tell you tomorrow. Over lunch?

Just getting back to work. Already have plans 4 tomorrow. Going to be busy.

Whoever was messing with me was slow on the response. Almost thought one wasn't coming. I went to turn off my phone again, tired of the games. Then it buzzed.

U might have plans 4 tomorrow. But who knows tomorrow's plans for u? N'est-ce pas?

I smiled, having no clue what it meant. But I liked it.

But tomorrow could wait because today was calling my ass back inside the courthouse.

9

I sat in our conference room, the impressive view of downtown Houston behind me, as I assisted Jacobi's depo prep—deposition preparation—of one of our clients. I sat at one end of the large mahogany table, looking at the police report in my hands as Jacobi, opposite me, asked the questions. The well-kept Latina cougar named Iris wasn't very believable in her version of facts yet. It was our job to change that. I resisted the urge to roll my eyes when Jacobi placed his hand atop hers to calm her down, feigning ignorance to the dazzling wedding ring she wore. Oh-so-empathetic; I'd seen this move before by him.

I received a text just as I was about to interject. Same number as yesterday that I didn't recognize.

Tomorrow's today. U still swamped with work?

Yes. As usual.

I replied to my anonymous jokester. Jacobi was right here, so it couldn't be him. Now my mind began racing with this distraction, wondering if perhaps it was a wrong number.

Even if I treat u to lunch?

Where?

I asked, knowing I was too busy, but allowing the amusing game to continue.

The Breakfast Klub.

U had me at hello. But I'm still in the middle of something.

Don't make me beg.

Who is this?

"Chase, do you have anything to add?" Jacobi asked, getting my attention. His hand still rested on our client's and she didn't seem to mind. The blank stare of my face probably had them both puzzled.

"No. I think you pretty much summed it up," I lied, looking up from my phone. Another buzz alerted me, compelling me to gaze downward once more.

I was rewarded for my devotion with a photo of a smiling Ava. Wow. I'd hoped it was her. The text that accompanied it read:

Take a break. I'll hold a seat 4 u . . . if u hurry.

I had many a question, like how did she get my cell phone number. But right now, I only had a desire to be there face-to-face.

I abruptly stood up, interrupting Jacobi as he stressed the importance of listening to his instructions during trial and not letting the defense get under Iris's skin. Right now, he'd rather be under her skin himself. I caught his attention, motioning randomly toward my head as if I were still addled from the car wreck and needed some air. He nodded for me to get out of there. As I left down the hall, I wondered if they'd be there when I returned or perhaps in some nearby hotel room pursuing a serious *debriefing* of one another.

As I cast silent aspersions, I reminded myself that I was no better hustling to rendezvous with some random female . . . for lunch.

On my way.

I texted, calculating how fast I could safely get there without risking another crash.

At least Jacobi was single.

I had no reason to heed the siren call in my head.

Yet I followed.

With no regard for the rocks ahead threatening to crash and submerge all I held dear.

10

Having a tiny rental car had its benefits. I swooped into a just- emptied parking spot on Travis and promptly hustled across the street to the Breakfast Klub, one of Houston's landmarks for good eats.

Here.

I texted as I searched the line of customers at the door for a glimpse of a face matching the one on my phone. Women at a table outside were selling purses with two interested patrons asking the prices as I walked by. I paused to acknowledge them as they glanced my way. A professional-looking brother in a nice suit garnered attention from the fairer sex most days.

Seated already.

Ava replied with a text of her own.

I eased past the line, receiving a scowl or two from hungry folk thinking I was cutting. Upon entering, I was overwhelmed by the sensory overload of spices and seasoning, instantly making my mouth water. I stepped aside, politely nodding at one of the passing staff as I looked for Ava. I found her seated alone, center table, with hair pulled back and Coach reading glasses to appear somewhat bookish. A singular point of calmness amid the commotion of people swirling all around her, plates of food being served about to the newly arrived as the recently satisfied left. When she recognized me, she waved. Far from vain, I felt self-conscious about the minute traces of my car wreck still etched in my face. Still, I waved back and came over.

Before I had a chance to sit, she stood up and hugged me tight. I held my breath this time, fear of coconut seduction haunting my dreams once again. When she kissed my cheek, I exhaled, throwing my resolve out the window. Damn my weakness. Despite her casual appearance today, Ava cast a spell over me and there was no denying it.

"Thank you for twisting my arm," I said as I gestured for her to return to her seat. She wore a jeweled print tank and form-fitting dark denim jeans, which I appreciated.

"Hope I didn't get you in any trouble."

"No. Just the normal tedious nature of things."

"Which you don't like," she added, more as a statement than an assumption. Ballsy.

"I didn't say that."

"You don't have to. I know these things," she said, tapping a single finger to her temple.

"So arguing is pointless?"

"*Oui, monsieur*. But I'll stop. When people push too much, you resist," she replied matter-of-factly as she put her cup of their signature Klub Karmel Machiatto to her lips. Made me think about Dawn's countless admonishments concerning my career. "You're healing up nicely," Ava said as she reached out and gently touched my face. I felt the electricity arc off her fingertips. That familiar tingling like that night at the pub. I wondered if any of other the restaurant-goers could sense it too.

"Yeah. Just a few scratches and bumps. I'm lucky," I said, wondering if I was referring to surviving the accident or simply meeting her.

"What did your wife say about my gift?"

"The painting? Oh. She didn't see it," I said not-so-truthfully. Damn concussion again. "I . . . accidentally left it at the hospital. Sorry."

"It's okay," she replied, an odd smile drifting across her face. "That one was kind of hurried, anyway. My stuff's usually less abstract."

I began to say something, but happened to look over her shoulder, noticing some of the artwork adorning the Breakfast Klub walls. They always exhibited local artists' work for their customers' appreciation as well as purchase. Several of the current pieces resembled the tiny memento given me by Ava. One of them had a piano in it too—a pair of little hands resting on its keys beside an older pair.

Interesting.

Fascinating.

Familiar. Yet I didn't know why.

"You were about to say something?"

"Uh . . . yes. How'd you get my number? I know I was dazed, but I'm sure I didn't give it to you. Didn't get the chance."

"Wondered when you'd ask," she said as she giggled. She positioned her order number on the table so it could be viewed easier by the waitstaff. "Chase, before I returned your phone to you at Memorial Hermann, I dialed my phone from yours. Just like you did when we first met. Some line about—"

"Fear of rejection," I answered for her.

Stunned.

Utterly stunned.

"You remember!" Ava gushed, color flooding her face and fire dancing in her eyes.

"Yeah," I answered with a nervous grin. I remembered that particular encounter at college. Except it never occurred with Ava. It was something I'd said to my wife Dawn when we first met. How did she know this? Now my not remembering Ava had become troubling on so many levels.

Before I could decide to address it, two plates of food were delivered to our table.

"I know you don't have much time, so I took the liberty of ordering for you. Hope you don't mind."

She pointed for the wings and waffle order to be placed in front of her. The other plate, the one with a cheezy 3 omelet and two biscuits, was for me. My favorite. All that was missing was . . .

"I already poured the hot syrup for your biscuits," she said, sliding the small maple-filled plastic container my way.

Too much. She had me spooked now. It was as if someone had given her a script. "Really. Who are you?" I asked, semi-serious.

"Chase!" someone called out from behind me before Ava could respond. She motioned for me to acknowledge whoever it was. I looked over my shoulder to see Jacobi and our client Iris as they sought an open table. It would be a funny coincidence if I didn't have to explain myself to my friend later. He grinned as he carried the number for his table's order, his eyes travelling between me and the woman with whom I sat. From my previous description of Ava to him, he had to know this was her. My mystery woman.

They stopped, leading me to think they were going to ask to sit with us. The look on my face begged him to spare me and not to ask. Nevertheless, I reached up to shake his hand.

"Hey, man. Early lunch too, huh?" I asked calmly as if my skating out on them back at the office were no big deal.

"Mrs—Iris here," Jacobi said, correcting himself at her insistence, "wanted some fresh air, so I suggested we grab a bite to eat. I see great minds think alike."

"Yes," I said, knowing the bite he wanted to eat was

Iris. I was trying to avoid similar thoughts of my face stuffed between Ava's legs at the moment, but wondered recklessly if she could deliver on the promises of my imagination.

"Hello. Jacobi Stewart," he said, shaking Ava's hand before I had a chance to willingly introduce them.

"I know you!" Iris blurted out from around Jacobi as she leaned in to get a better view of Ava. At least somebody remembered her. "It's been a couple of years, hasn't it?"

"Yes. You're right," Ava answered nervously, something unspoken between the two of them. "How've you been, Iris?"

"I'm doing good these days. Real good," Iris replied. "These fine young men are helping me with my case."

"Yes, so if you ever need a good law firm, call us. Or just call Chase here," Jacobi said to Ava as he placed his hand on my shoulder. "I still didn't get your name, miss."

"Charla Nuttier," Iris answered for her enthusiastically. "You've never heard of her? I have several of her paintings. Incredible artist," she said to Jacobi.

"Thank you. You're too kind," the woman who told me her name was Ava replied. "Actually, some of my other works are on the wall here," she said to both of them, confirming my earlier suspicions. I looked at the paintings again. She was an impressive artist and even more an enigma than before.

"I'll have to check them out, ma'am," Jacobi stated. "It was nice meeting you."

As Jacobi and Iris darted for a freshly open table, I stared at Ava, who seemed uncomfortable with the attention. And why did Iris know her by a different name? We began eating our food with me enjoying this simple time with Ava. But she kept Iris in her sights, pausing from her chews whenever Iris spoke to Jacobi and looked her way. Suddenly, she dropped her fork mid-meal. "I have to go, Chase," she said.

"But you didn't finish your food," I blurted out , relishing the meal she'd bought me.

"I know. I have to go, though."

"Well, let me walk you out."

"You don't have to," she said, suddenly trying to distance herself from me as if I no longer interested her. She fetched her purse from beneath the table, then excused herself. I left a tip, hastily taking a final bite of my syrup-drenched biscuit, then followed in pursuit.

"Charla Nuttier? Why does she know you by that name?" I asked, overtaking her in the parking lot. My stomach still yearned for my half-finished omelet and the other biscuit left abruptly at our table inside. The lawyerly part of me had many questions, but this was the most immediate one at the moment.

"It's the name I do my work under. Allows me freedom."

"And allows you to remain a mystery," I said, my turn to play know-it-all. "Any more I'm supposed to know, Ava?"

"Yes. Lots. Just not here," she sang, her interest back.

"Uh-huh. Do you need a ride wherever it is you're in such a hurry to be?"

She shifted gears, breaking from the pace she'd begun. She reached up, gripping my arm as she pulled herself up to my lips. Contact. The kiss was soft, sensual, but teased of more ravenous wants. "No. I'll be fine, Chase," she said, patting my chest as if subconsciously talking herself out of something reckless . . . for now. "Thank you for coming when I called. I needed to see you."

"Hey. Can't promise I'll drop everything in the future

if you call," I threw out there blindly with a shrug of my shoulders.

"You don't have to promise, Chase. You have my number now. Maybe I'll be the one to come running. In fact, I can almost guarantee it."

Rather than going to my car or returning inside, I watched Ava as she walked away. Stood there, fixated, until I couldn't see her anymore.

Then I stored the number in my phone under the name of Charla Nuttier, creator of fine works. For as beautiful as her paintings were, she was the true work of art.

11

"Was that your mysterious stalker lady friend?" Jacobi asked, having returned extra late from his lunch with our client Iris. Satisfied, he sat down, then put his feet up on my desk. I turned my attention away from my computer monitor, knowing I'd get no work done while he was in here.

"She's not a stalker. But yeah . . . that was her."

"*Niiiiice*. Bet if she took them eyeglasses off . . ." he said, his voice fading as he squinted his eyes to focus on his dark thoughts. "Anyway. I can see why you'd bail on us. Did she refresh your memory yet?"

"No, but Iris sure seems to know her."

"Yeah. I caught that. Figured I'd pry for you. She told me they used to see the same therapist. So I might be right about her being a stalker. When you do go by her place, be sure to check her closet for shrines to you and remove all knives from the kitchen. That is, unless you've already been to her place."

"No," I said drily. "And I'm trying to avoid that."

"Bruh, you don't have to bullshit me. I saw that busted look on your face back at Breakfast Klub. You want to hit it and she wants you to hit it. In the worst way, I might add."

"Man, what am I doing?" I said, putting my face in my hands and letting out a deep breath.

"If it's stressing you that much, allow me to take that load off your hands. I can say I remember her from band camp or something."

"It's not just the physical shit with this woman. It's a big city, man. If something like this was on my mind, I could've done it a long time ago. This . . . this is something else and I couldn't explain it if I tried. I don't know how, but it's like she gets me."

"You sure your dick isn't trying to rationalize this by making it deeper than what it really is? Face it. She's hot, she's mysterious, and she's feeling you. On most days, for most men, that would do the trick."

"After my wreck, she rode with me in the ambulance, man. I was foolishly looking for her when it happened. Stayed by my side at Memorial Hermann until you and Dawn arrived. It's like she cares. Feels genuine."

"Okay. Maybe it's misplaced appreciation on your part. Ever thought about that?"

"No. Just wish I could remember her from back in college. At the Breakfast Klub, she mentioned things I never did with her. Only Dawn. And she knows my favorite food over there too. Ordered it for me before I even told her anything."

"Uh-huh," Jacobi muttered. "Maybe there's a reason you don't remember this girl. You never met her before."

"*Ooookay.* But I don't know what you're getting at."

"Dawn, bro," he scolded. He took his feet down, then leaned forward so as to avoid anyone overhearing what he was about to say. "What I'm saying is that maybe, just maybe, Dawn is doing this. Either testing you or wants to get leverage on you . . . for a divorce."

"Dude, you're crazy. Dawn wouldn't do something like that. Besides, if she wanted a divorce, she'd just file. I don't have shit in terms of assets anyway."

"But does *she* have assets? Hmm? Easier to make you the bad guy if she's thinking about leaving and wants to protect what she feels is hers. C'mon, we've seen everything in our line of work. I hate to think like that, but I'm trying to be honest here."

"That doesn't fly, man. I was the one who approached Ava."

"*Ava?*" Jacobi asked with a grimace. "I thought Iris said her name was Charla Nuttier or something to that effect."

"Whatever. Anyway, I approached her outside the pub. Not the other way around."

"But pretty convenient for her to show up all alone at the same place as you. Maybe Dawn knew exactly where you were. Just dangling the bait for the fish to bite. Chomp."

"And I was out drinking with you. Maybe Dawn is paying you to put me in these bad situations," I said, joking as I turned the tables.

"Not funny, man. I certainly hope I'm wrong with my theories, but don't want you getting blindsided. Besides, if you tell Dawn I came up with this, I'll deny it. One of us on her bad side is enough."

If Jacobi was aware of my wife's less-than-stellar assessment of him, he didn't acknowledge it to me. "Thanks for your concern," I responded, knowing he'd put a lot on my plate for me to digest.

12

I looked at the name Charla Nuttier on my phone, debating over whether to call or delete it—especially after Jacobi shared his theories with me. I could just let it all go and move on. Safe, I suppose in that ignorance of what could be or what might be going on maybe being bliss in this situation. I decided to postpone that debate for another time and exited the Chevy Aveo. For another woman demanded my attention at the moment.

I walked onto the porch of the single-story, white-framed home on West Montgomery Road and knocked twice, my usual code. As I patiently waited, I watched a lady exit Family Affair beauty shop next door. She stopped and checked her fresh new do in the reflection of her tan Cadillac DeVille's tinted windows. As she made minute hair adjustments with her fingers, she suddenly turned and waved at me. Good eyes to go along with the nice full breasts apparent under her T-shirt.

"Heeeey!" she said, pearly whites gleaming.

"Hey," I said, politely waving back as was required. Southern politeness and all.

Just as she began to mouth something else, a man who I assume was her boyfriend exited the barbershop, carrying a little boy with a fresh cut. She quickly turned away as if I were no longer there, hastily entering the Caddy's passenger seat. He placed the young child in the backseat, pausing to stare me down for some perceived slight.

Never a dull moment in Acres Homes.

I turned my attention back to the front door that was opening with the shuffle of multiple door locks and security chains. A diminutive yet deceptively strong woman greeted me, her deep brown skin bearing the creases and lines from years of hard work and circumstances. Her shock of thinning silver-gray hair hung freely, undone from the neat little bun she kept it in while cleaning office buildings. She still wore her uniform, but had nestled into her favorite pair of slippers. I'd tried over the years to get her to stop working and take it easy. Futility. Work was her therapy.

"Your paper," I said, handing the folded copy of the *Houston Chronicle* to my mother Earnestine as she allowed me to enter her home. The humble abode, my grandmother's previously, had been in the family several generations. The only time it was vacant was the brief period when my parents tried to make a go of it.

And we knew how that turned out.

Lucky for us that she didn't sell it.

"Where's your car?" she asked, glancing at my tiny rental parked behind her old burgundy Chevy Malibu.

"Gone. That's a rental. Had a minor accident."

"Don't sound minor to me, boy. You okay?"

"I'm fine, Mom. Didn't want to worry you with it. How was your day?"

"Same as the day before. My feet a little more sore, though."

"Did you use that gift certificate for the pedicure yet?"

"No. I don't like people playin' with my feet, boy. That's personal."

"If you're not gonna use it, I can give it to Dawn," I teased. She gave me a playful tap on the shoulder, knowing she wasn't one to part with a gift, even if it would go unused. I reciprocated by kissing her on the cheek and giving her a big hug.

"How is that wife of yours, baby?" she asked.

"She's good, Mom. She asked about you the other day. Wants to have you over for dinner," I answered as I walked into the kitchen and opened the refrigerator. It was lacking quite a bit, just as the cabinets, I'd bet. "When was the last time you went to the store?" I asked.

"A week or so. Been too busy. And you know I don't leave once I'm in for the night."

"That's why I stopped by. Get your purse. I'm taking you by Wal-Mart . . . before it gets dark."

"You don't have to do that, boy. I can take myself."

"And I don't doubt it, but I insist." Last time she went by the Wal-Mart on I-45, she almost got jacked on the parking lot. Security actually did its job and ran off the person before things got crazy. But I wasn't letting her go there by herself ever again.

"In that little-bitty thing?" she asked, her face contorting over the rental car in the driveway. Her Malibu may have been larger, but it was hardly in better shape.

"Yes, ma'am. It's bigger on the inside. Crazy space-age styling. Trust me," I joked.

"Hmph. I guess," she said, relenting.

On our way to Wal-Mart, I stopped at North Shepherd, waiting to make a left turn. "Saw Dad the other day," I offered without taking my eyes off the road.

"Oh? How's he look?" my mother inquired, her curiosity less than subdued. This was how the two communicated with one another. Indirectly and anecdotally through the one thing not destroyed by their union: Me. I was the carrier pigeon.

"Y'know," I offered, letting her fill in the rest. "He asked about you."

"And?"

"I told him you were good." *Just as you've been the whole time without him*, I thought. At one time, Joell Hidalgo was more than a street urchin, entertaining the few that stopped to appreciate his magic. He was once magic itself—a legendary jazz musician and front man for the Asylum Seekers. Before the demons in his head and within the bottle consumed him. Even those my mother would've tolerated, if not for the endless womanizing that made things unbearable. I was almost in my teens when I came to learn all the sordid details. Mouthy drunk relatives at reunions say the darndest things—sometimes altering the course of stuff in unexpected ways.

"He needs to take care of himself rather than worrying about me," my mother spouted, even though it was obvious she appreciated his interest even if from afar. We'd reached West Little York and took a right to take us to I-45. I passed the Popeyes chicken on the right- hand side, taking a left beneath the overpass on the green light, speeding up on the feeder road—as best I could—to merge onto the freeway.

"Was he the one for you?" I asked as we passed the McDonald's followed by a crowded Food Town grocery store.

"Huh? You usually not one to talk about that," she said with a giggle I was unaccustomed to hearing. It gave me a glimpse into that fresh-faced girl who was first swept off her feet by the smooth, pretty *Cubano* music man decades past. "I think so. Problem was he was the one for a bunch of others too."

I didn't discuss it further, but wondered how I could feel that Dawn was the one yet be drawn to Ava in such a similar fashion. But maybe my mother had spelled it out for me. I was my father's son, after all. And for as much as I did to avoid being anything like him, perhaps fate had other plans.

13

Back at home, I decided to do some research, but different from my legal pursuits by day. I figured maybe I could learn as much about Ava as she knew about me. Dawn was in the kitchen checking on her gumbo, so I used that time to slip into the home office. Not having a last name, I quickly pulled up Google on my laptop and entered the only full name I had associated with Ava-Charla Nuttier.

A few entries popped up in the search results that matched what I was looking for. The most relevant one looked to be from an online *Houston Style* article referring to an unusual new artist who suddenly burst onto the scene over a year ago. Dawn entered the office, looking over my shoulder as I clicked on the entry. I didn't hesitate, quietly observing her for any signs of deceit or nervousness.

"Ever heard of her?" I asked of Dawn as the woman I knew as Ava filled the screen, one of her larger paintings on display behind her. It was like that of New York City, yet with the Twin Towers intact, but different. The architecture was simultaneously familiar yet otherworldly, including the strange sailboats on the Hudson River.

"No," Dawn replied, resting an elbow on my shoulder. Her face passive, but showing interest in the article I was perusing. It stated that the mysterious Charla Nuttier's paintings seemed to be, as quoted from the review, *inspired from the most mundane parts in the life of a child to voices from worlds beyond our own, but with both equally reminding us of our humanity*. That was all we were allowed to read without being a subscriber to the magazine's premium content.

"You sure you don't know her?" I asked again while she stared at Ava's image. Felt a bit like I was deposing my own wife.

"I'm positive. Why?"

"I dunno. Figured as a new artist in the area that you might've heard of her. Your sort of thing."

"Nope, but her stuff looks interesting and eclectic. Thinking about buying some pieces for the house? Didn't peg you as an art man."

"I'm not, but it catches the eye. Saw some of her more 'regular' stuff on display in the Breakfast Klub," I mumbled, fixated more on the artist than the article. "Hmm. Don't know her by name, but her face looks familiar. Like maybe she went to college with us."

Dawn leaned over me, her eyes narrowing in response to my observation. "Nope. Don't remember seeing her on campus. But she is very beautiful. Don'tcha think, baby?"

"She's cute, I suppose," I said, carefully treading the minefield of a spouse's goading. Was she simply kidding or was there something more sinister? Was everything just what it seemed or was there something entirely different bearing out in our conversation? Thanks, Jacobi, for making me distrustful of my wife.

My phone, which rested on the desk, buzzed suddenly. Not a call, but a text. It was from Ava. I quickly moved away from Dawn's line of sight, guilt eating away at me.

"Jacobi," I said with a sigh. She was used to that sort of intrusion.

"More work?"

"I'll let you guess."

"I'm going check on the gumbo," Dawn said with an apparent eye roll. "You hungry?"

"Starving," I responded with a smile.

I turned to read the message before she'd taken two steps.

> You didn't call.
>
> Wasn't going to.

I hastily replied.

> Ur scared. I can understand that. So am I.
>
> Of what?
>
> Rejection. Don't know what I would do.
>
> Don't know what I'm doing. Have 2 ask u something.
>
> Been waiting for that.
>
> U might not like it.
>
> K. Do it in person then.
>
> Tomorrow?
>
> Unless I can c u 2nite.
>
> Ha. Ha. Cute.
>
> That you are.
>
> Have 2 go.
>
> K. I have so much to say. But I'll wait. But not much longer. Xoxo.

I smiled, quickly deleting any traces of my conversation with Ava. Hot gumbo was waiting for me in the kitchen and my appetite was whetted. But it would be tomorrow before it was either sated or soured. Options I neither expected nor asked for. For everything has a price, whether we can afford it or not.

14

Her directions were perfect, even down to which parking spots would be vacant at this time of day.

My hand trembled as I buzzed Ava's unit. I was here an hour later than I'd promised. But my doubts had scored a fleeting victory. Tried to stay away, but couldn't. A foolish man driven by something beyond his understanding. A fresh breeze kicked up, rustling the leaves on the full oaks that dotted the sidewalk in front of her townhome. I adjusted my tie that felt more like a noose.

"It's open," she replied over the speaker without even asking who it was.

"It's me, by the way. Don't want you thinking it's some killer or something," I joked, more for my benefit. A loser's levity.

"I know," she said softly, her mad sexy voice reverberating through the intercom. "And if it wasn't you, I would prefer not to live anyway. Now . . . come on up." Her words chilled me. Blind, undiluted passion for me evident in every sweet syllable. Perhaps Jacobi's suggestion that I check her closets for shrines wasn't far off course.

I crossed the threshold of her home onto the deep-stained cherrywood floor; noticed the soft candlelight and calming piano music next. Could imagine returning here from a hard day's work in another life, perhaps. As my apprehension eased, I smiled at her, trying to ignore the seductive atmosphere. Ava seemed perturbed by my lack of punctuality, but handed me a glass of wine anyway. I held the non-stemmed tumbler, moving the white wine in tight circles before putting it to my nose. I took a sip, recognizing the familiar dry texture on my tongue as Gewürztraminer, a particular favorite of mine among the German wines. Another in a string of way too many coincidences with this woman. What was next? A fresh new pack of my favorite underwear atop her bed?

She closed the door, standing between me and any sure means of escape. Taking another sip, I took in her magnificence. Ava wore her tresses pinned back, dazzling diamond earrings hanging from her lobes. The short, black silk asymmetric dress gorgeously accentuated her frame while revealing a single bare shoulder. She drank of her wine and cut her eyes at me as though I were wounded prey. Damn seductive. Felt like I needed to smoke a cigarette just from my thoughts.

"Wow," I said, raising my glass in a toast. I took a few discreet breaths, to try to maintain my composure, but could feel my heart revving unrestrained.

"The wine? You're lucky I kept it chilled," she teased.

"I was referring to it . . . and you. And I apologize for being late, but I have to ask you something." Had to focus just to get it out, but was glad I did.

"Ah, yes. The infamous question you've been dying to ask." She swirled her wine around this time, grinning as she looked into her glass, then back at me. "I'm all ears."

"Did my wife put you up to this?"

"Excuse me?" she replied, disgusted. Apparently not the question she was expecting. Score one for my surprising her. "I don't even know this woman. Are you kettled?"

"*Kettled*? I'm lost."

"Um . . . drunk," she explained. "Sorry. Some of the words here are different."

"Here? You mean in Houston?"

Ava chuckled, but some hint of anger at herself due to that strange phrase was still evident. Odd. "Yes. I was living somewhere else before arriving here," she replied with another strange choice of words. "And some of those habits are hard to shake. Forgive me."

"No big deal. But I still need to know. Do you know my wife?" I asked.

"No," she said with a slight flare of her nostrils. Animosity was there, but was it from my question or the mention of Dawn? I watched her chest rise. Could tell her heart was racing too.

"You say you went to Sam Houston State with me. Well, so did my wife. Dawn Henderson was her maiden name," I pushed on as she came closer. Watched her lick her lips while trying not to lick mine.

"I never heard of her, Chase. And truth be told, don't particularly care to know about her at the moment. I'm here for you, baby. Just you. No games." With that said, she downed the remainder of her wine and placed her tumbler on the table beside her.

I stared at her in silence for a moment. Debating if, despite my believing her, whether I should simply walk away. But could I? "No games?" I asked.

"No games," she said, walking into my grasp. "I just want you to tell me you want me . . . tell me you need me." I placed my free hand on her ass, pulling her closer. As we came together, I inhaled. Coconut was in the air again, intoxicating me more than the glass in hand ever could. I never knew I liked this smell so much until I met Ava.

"I want you. I need you. I do, I do. Gawd, you smell so good," I said, my lips grazing hers. She wouldn't be disappearing down the street or into the night this time.

"If you like the smell, wait 'til you get a taste," she

said, giving herself up to me. "Taste me, Chase. Please. Taste every part of me."

She pried the wineglass away from me, allowing me to fully grope her ass. I slid my hands under the silk, firmly squeezing her roundness as if each cheek were a stress ball. With each grip, she gasped. I blew into Ava's ear as she bit at my shoulder through my shirt.

"I can't believe you're here," she mouthed.

"I am, though," I said, exhilarated and stunned by the turn of events leading to this moment.

I dropped to my knees, lifting the short front of her dress and exposing her inviting thong. She shuddered as I plunged my face between her legs, pheromones guiding me to her pussy as if it were a beacon for my unleashed lust. As I moved her thong aside, tickling her clit with my tongue, her body squirmed and shimmied.

"Yes! Yes! Chase, oh you're sooo good. Mmmm," Ava gushed as she came for me. The newness of it all was driving me crazy, making me a frenzied fool. I stood back up and lifted her off her feet, biting and sucking on her neck as we spun round and round. Despite being caught up in the moment, I lowered her back down to the floor. Tried to find my moral true north amidst a swirling sea of desire.

"I—I'm married, Ava. My wife—" I offered in a labored breath, closing my eyes as I tried in vain to picture Dawn. The bulge in my slacks was noticeable. Probably had been from when I first came in the door. I felt her hand as she began to stroke me. She tugged on my zipper, her deft fingers masterfully coaxing my dick free with ease. As it tumbled from my pants, it was my turn to groan and beg.

"I'm your wife tonight," she whispered breathlessly before kissing me. As our lips touched and tongues joined, I knew I'd lost—lost before I'd even pressed that buzzer.

Lost when I felt the crackle of electricity beneath a street-light.

And by the noose around my neck, she led me to her bedroom where she continued to show me what a wife can do.

15

Ava lay atop me, sweet sticky sweat clinging between us as I held onto her waist. She gave me the tip of her tongue, teasing me as it darted in and out of my open mouth. When I caught it, I gently sucked, our passion intermingling. Somehow she found the energy for another session, working her hips up and down, moaning as I filled her yet again. She reared up, giving her breasts to me, which I grasped and began to lather with kisses, swollen nipples hardening against my eager lips.

"Oh!" she exclaimed as I nipped at her. Her intensity picked up as she came again and again, her intoxicating moistness enveloping me. As she rode me toward another gusher, I looked into her eyes, having been assured that her tears were those of joy. I rolled her onto her back, knocking sheets aside as I proceeded to quicken my pace and take charge of this maddening ride. She dug her nails into my back, gasping as I thrust deeper inside her honey-coated walls. I throbbed and bobbed to her rhythm, surprised by how two unfamiliar bodies could be in sync with one another. Fascinating.

"You—you're—damn!" I blurted out as sweat dripped from me, the monster deep in my loins threatening to burst free.

"Oooh. I've missed you so much, my love," she uttered with delight.

I gasped, startled out my groove by her comment.

But she urged me to continue, her hips swaying and surging upward as if a tsunami wave threatening to overwhelm me.

"Don't stop. Please," she said, her eyes desperately pleading for more of what I had to bestow. I became lost in those damned eyes. And the monster in my loins growled again. I resumed my motion, giving in to it. Letting the beast take control of me. Living at that moment as if I were her lover. Ava nodded, her eyes meeting mine as I surged. She wrapped her legs around me, preventing any escape from her unyielding love.

"I—I'm—I'm about to—" I stammered. Her pussy was so good.

"Don't stop. Don't stop," she cooed as her hands pressed against my chest. She smiled as if not really here, but caught up in a spell. When I felt her warm eruption again, I lost it as well. I wouldn't—couldn't—escape Ava if I wanted to. I grunted as I came. And the monster in my loins lurched free, unfettered of any misgivings or scant reluctance still left in me.

Our bodies pressed together violently as I erupted inside her. My body went limp from the climax as my eyes rolled back in my head. Ava trembled as she let out a low moan. The only person I'd climaxed so hard with before was Dawn. And at this moment, that was questionable.

For what seemed an eternity, neither of us spoke. Trying to allow reason and normal functions to return, I suppose. We were marionettes with cut strings, our bodies forming a naked heap of consumed emotion and spent desires.

Eventually, I found the strength to roll off of her and check the time on my watch. I had to go . . . even if the guilt hadn't begun creeping in. Ava opened her eyes, her smile of rabid insanity replaced by that of an angel.

"Stay. I don't want you to leave," she said as she dragged a fingernail across my thigh.

"It's not that simple. I'm married," I responded, trying to solve the puzzle of where each piece of my clothing lay. My shirt hung partially off the nightstand, draped across a book of Ava's—*Parallel Univ erses* by Fred Alan Wolf. That stuff was a little heady for me, but different tastes for different people.

"Yes. I recall your saying that before. Right before we fucked . . . the first time."

I smiled to acknowledge my appreciation "You?" I asked.

"What?"

"Married?" I asked. Can't say I'd bothered checking for a wedding ring.

"I was."

"Was. Divorce?" I sat up as I prepared to get dressed, retrieving my slacks and underwear off the carpet.

"No. I'm a widow. He passed away. Unexpectedly."

"Oh. Sorry to hear that," I said, lowering my voice. I wondered if he'd shared this very bed with her.

"I wound up here not long afterward."

"Needed a change of scenery? An escape from the memories?" I asked, pausing from my dressing to take her hand. Made me remember what our client Iris said to Jacobi about sharing therapists with Ava. Maybe it was to help her deal with the grief. Totally understandable.

"No. I didn't plan it. Coming here was sudden . . . totally unexpected. I just wanted him back so bad. I never knew what brought me here—or why—until I saw you outside the pub. And I don't go out much. But it was like something drew me there that night. That's when it all made sense."

"So you went to Sam Houston State in Huntsville

with me, but you never came to Houston until after your husband died?" I found it odd, but not totally unimaginable. Maybe she was from Dallas or something.

"It's complicated," Ava offered, sitting up in the bed. "I'll share it with you. Maybe when you have more time." My leaving was still smarting to her. As I looked at this hauntingly beautiful woman, a hollow feeling formed inside at the thought of walking out that door. But I had to. Being here . . . and doing this, while instinctual and so natural, was wrong.

"Where are you from?" I asked, giving up on trying to remember her from college.

"A little town in Louisiana. Pouppeville." she answered. Jacobi was at least right about that. She was one of those Louisiana girls.

"Pouppeville? Never heard of it."

"Yeah. I get that a lot," she said with a chuckle to herself.

"Can I ask you something else?" I floated while putting my tie back on. It smelled of her as did the rest of my clothes. One of many reasons I never considered cheating on Dawn until now. Too many problems like this to manage.

"Please do. I want you to know me as I know you," Ava replied. Odd phrasing. Almost as if she'd lived abroad.

"No offense, but am I a rebound or something to make up for your husband?"

She reflected on it for a moment, but calmly answered, "No. You are more than that, Chase. I don't know how much time I have here. But you are for me. I know it in my heart. If anything, my husband's death reminded me to not take second chances for granted."

"Did you love him?"

"With all my heart."

"Was he an artist too? I've been doing some research on Charla Nuttier, but there's not a lot out there."

"No," she replied with a giggle as she rose from the bed. "He was a musician."

I followed Ava as she boldly bounded, unclothed, down the hallway. I grinned at the jiggle of her ass cheeks and her total comfort with me. "What did he play?" I asked. I knew dwelling on him wasn't a good thing, but I was putting forth the effort to learn something about her beyond my odd feelings and her being sensational in bed.

"He was a pianist. Famous," she said, coming to a halt before entering the living room. She turned to look into my eyes. Had to see the surprise in them.

"Wow. I used to play the piano," I offered, not quite sure why I would volunteer such a thing.

"Do you still play?"

"No," I answered abruptly. "And I was far from famous. Stopped a long time ago."

"Why?" she asked, appearing shaken by my admission.

"I have my reasons," I replied. "Like you said, maybe we'll talk about it when I have more time."

"Very well," Ava said, seemingly satisfied that we'd have other times to ourselves. It pleased me too. She finished walking me to her door, where she held her arms out for a hug. Both of us knew that wasn't how this would end as I stepped closer. We kissed madly, like glowing schoolkids on a second date, before I pried myself away. She relented, unlocking the front door and stepping aside. I gripped the door frame on my way out and turned to say my formal good-byes.

"When?" she asked, speaking through the space in her door to where passersby couldn't enjoy the sights I was beholding.

"We'll see," I replied, my head swirling as I went about preparing for my trip home.

Back to my car, I called Jacobi.

"What up, man?" he answered.

"Hey. If Dawn asks, we were playing racquetball to-day after work."

"So you actually did it, huh?" he responded.

"Yes."

"How was it?"

"Good," I replied, understating things after a pause.

"Uh-huh. Why do I get the feeling this is more than a HIQI," he said, using his infamous acronym for hit-it-and-quit-it situations.

"Dude, responding to that isn't worth the trouble for either of us."

"Chase, I love you like a brother, but be careful. This kind of game ain't for you."

"Duly noted, sir. And thanks," I said, ending the conversation.

Her husband played the piano too. Don't know why that bothered me so much. Probably a different family situation growing up. But life is still about choices. Maybe deep down, I wished that painting Ava had given me had personal significance when it was done. But, anyway, how could she know I used to play the piano? That was something Dawn was oblivious to also.

Ego.

But she'd stroked more than that today anyway, I thought with a wry smile.

I'd have a lot to consider and assess on my way home, but first I had to shed my clothes and get them to a dry cleaner's ASAP.

16

"How was racquetball?" Dawn queried as I returned home. She stood at the kitchen island, positioned as if a store mannequin before the granite countertop as she worked on her notebook computer. She still wore her blouse and skirt from a long day at Macy's, but was answering e-mail from her college prep business. As she click-clacked away in response, she scratched an itch on her calf with the other foot, her blue Steve Madden pumps resting on their sides where she'd discarded them.

"Too long," I answered, having recently felt the sting from Ava's scratches on my back as I exited the car. My stomach lurched as pangs of guilt swept over me. I wished Dawn had worked until closing tonight. Would've given me a better chance of gathering myself.

"Did you win?" she asked. She pushed her laptop away from the island's edge then came closer. I knew my wife's mannerisms well enough. Seduction was on her mind, but she never had to work hard at it with me. I was always willing, except for tonight. Things were different. Changed. I was marked with another woman's essence, our DNA having intermingled.

"No, but it was close," I answered with an exaggerated display of frustration, just as I felt the smarting reminder of Ava on my back again. "I just want to shower and go to bed. Facing Jacobi in the morning will be unbearable. And that's not counting the grief until our rematch."

"Oh. Maybe I can take your mind off things," she said, her eyes narrowing and her voice became more playful.

"You don't wanna do that," I said as I waved an arm, scrunching my face to enforce my message. "I reek. And had some *taco cabana* too. Whoo!" I fanned the air for further effect.

Dawn couldn't help but laugh as she backed away, her nose crinkling. "You don't have to tell me twice. I know what those chicken flautas and *pico de gallo* do to you. Hurry up and get in the shower, boy."

"Okay," I said, leaning in just enough to kiss her on the cheek and hoping she didn't smell the absence of what I conveyed. My supposed sweaty gym clothes were fresh, having hastily changed into them at a Chevron station off I-45 before dropping my sex-permeated gear at the dry cleaner's.

The shower wasn't fully warmed before I entered, rapidly foaming up my washcloth with sport-scented shower gel. Nerves still frayed, I vigorously scrubbed over every part of my body, as if I could shed my sins like a second skin. I'd given into the illusion of freedom, full-on, despite knowing deep down that something was off beyond obvious moral issues of what I had done. As the flow of water hit me in the face, I lamented spurning my wife's affections while wrongly reflecting on the other woman I'd touched, kissed, caressed, tasted, and pleasured repeatedly today.

When I turned off the shower and exited, things were still silent on the other side of the bathroom door. I locked it, examining the scratches on my back more closely in the mirror. They didn't look as noticeable as they felt, but were a valid reminder of my stupidity. After drying off, I applied a quick dab of Neosporin across it, then threw on a T-shirt for bed.

I tried to will myself to sleep, but kept reliving memories of another bed. Kept seeing Ava expressing her satisfaction as she sat atop my face, threatening to drown me in her love. I sniffed deeply of the hairs on my upper lip, ensuring that all was left from that was the memory of it. The clock on my nightstand only served to remind me that barely a minute had passed since my last glance at it. Frustrating. As I lay there, I unknowingly slipped into a deep sleep. I hadn't realized it until Dawn joined me in the bed, pulling the sheets back on her side. I was startled awake, not knowing how exhausted I was. I'd probably been snoring.

"You awake?" she asked as I felt her bare leg on mine across the gulf.

"Kinda," I replied as my voice cracked. "What's up?"

"Something wrong?"

"Besides the usual?" I responded, commenting on our ever- present tension over my career advancement.

"Yes."

"Nothing."

"You sure?" she asked as she slid closer. I remained deathly still.

"Yeah. I'm sure," I replied, telling myself there was no way Dawn and Ava were conspiring, even if it felt Ava had been fed information on me. "It's just been a long day." Long day—the accepted marital code loosely translated as: *No. We ain't fucking tonight.* Through our marriage, I'd been the only recipient of this coded dismissal before. I wasn't quite sure how my spouse would take being on the receiving end of such an affront.

I shut my eyes again; trying to flee back to the land of REM, for it would protect me. Keep me from revealing my guilt. I could feel Dawn's eyes blistering my skin in the dark. Wondered what ill thoughts were hatching inside that head of hers. Her next action was a long sigh, frustration totally evident.

"Hey," I said, daring to communicate again as I yawned. "What do you think about a cruise? We could leave out of Galveston next week. That would be a nice getaway, don'tchathink? Or maybe a run over to San Antonio and do the Riverwalk for a few days? " Maybe time away with Dawn would give me some clarity. Give me a moment to regroup and salvage this.

"I can't do that, Chase," she replied, her body's movement in the bed not betraying any reaction to my proposal. "I just posted my SAT classes on the Web site. Testing season is full underway. Are you trying to make up for something?"

"No, babe. Not at all," I said, my voice lowering second by second as I feigned drifting away again. While pretending to sleep, I heard Dawn as she reached for her nightstand drawer. After another long moment of silence, she sighed again.

Then I felt the faint vibrations as Dawn's sigh was replaced by low murmurs and moans. I felt a minute sway through the mattress, growing to a distinct, noticeable motion. Despite that, Dawn tried to control her trembling legs as she brought herself to climax at the hands of her magic bullet. I knew she'd used it from time to time, but that didn't make me any more comfortable that she was having to resort to this. For what seemed an eternity of building and subsiding, only to repeat again, Dawn let a deep gasp escape her throat as she buried her face in her pillow.

Then all was still again.

And the whole time I laid there, turned over, eyes tightly closed, pretending to be oblivious.

Just as I hoped Dawn was to me and what I had done.

17

I voluntarily relieved our courier of his duties today, running documents by the courthouse in his stead. Of course, my return to the office somehow brought me to Ava's place. A bear in search of honey. This time, though, I came unannounced.

As I approached the intercom to ring her, I observed a man exiting her door. The tall, gaunt fellow wore a pair of Ray·Ban aviators, which concealed his eyes, and a heavy brown trench coat— a bit too much for the mild weather we were experiencing. Gave the impression of a vampire hiding from an unyielding sun. Rather than proceed with pressing the button, I walked toward him. We met at the bottom of her steps where we exchanged looks.

"Hello," the thin-faced man with a wisp of blondish white hair said, his older, lined face revealing neither intimidation nor antagonism. He held out his hand, obliging me to take it.

"Hello," I offered in kind, unsure of my feelings toward the stranger whose hand I was shaking. I knew with whom he'd just visited and wondered if he'd ever delighted in Ava's smile . . . or more. Then he broke into an odd grin, snapping me out of my rabid speculation.

"You must be Chase."

"Yes," I responded flatly. Who in the fuck was he to know my name?

The stranger chuckled to himself. "Smith Sampson," he offered. A name reserved for either an aristocrat or porn star. Probably the former, I supposed, from the look of things. Of course I could be completely wrong. "I can't believe Ava found you."

"Ava," I echoed, seeing red that this man not only knew about me, but knew her by her real name. I was married, so it shouldn't have mattered. But it did. I chuckled then. My turn. Two roosters having a jolly old crow-off on the steps of the henhouse. And what did he mean by her finding me? "You don't use her pseudonym," I said, continuing.

"That Charla Nuttier thing? Heavens no," he said with a scoff. He laughed again, making me feel insignificant when I'd come here to feel important. To relish in feeling . . . special. Like maybe I could make the right choices in someone's eyes. "Can't say Ava doesn't have a sense of humor with that one. Well, I must be off. Things to do. It was nice meeting you, sir. Ava's a very special lady . . . as I'm sure you know."

"Take care," I said as I stepped aside. I waited for several seconds before ambling up the stairs to Ava's door. Before knocking, I took one final look at the man, this Smith Sampson, as he walked to the black BMW 750 taking up two parking spaces. I yearned to know Ava better than he. Then I knocked on her door, two short raps from my knuckles.

The door swung open wildly, Ava in mid-conversation before I could see her. "You forgot something?" she asked, being startled. "Oh. Hey, Chase!"

"Can I come in?"

"Of course. I didn't know you were coming over," she said, wrapping her arms around me. She smiled from behind those bookish Coach glasses of hers, wearing a tunic smeared with dried paint., which eased my ran-

dom thoughts about her visitor Smith for the moment.
We kissed before I abruptly ended it.

"Yeah. Missed you. You busy?" I asked, withholding
the bottled-up affection I held for her.

"For you? Never. I was just in the middle of therapy."

"Therapy?" I asked, remembering what Jacobi had
said and wondering if the thin, older man I'd met outside was more doctor than love doctor.

"My painting," she said, motioning me to follow her
to a room I hadn't been in before.

"Oooh," I gasped for effect, having my opening.
"When you said *therapy*, I thought you meant like
psychological. And that the man I met on your steps
was . . ." I held it out there on the wind from my lips,
leaving it to her to clarify.

"You met Smith? He's my patron, silly," she said, shaking her head. She continued, "What did he tell you?"

"Nothing really," I replied. Ava grasped the door handle, pausing to analyze my statement and assess what
my eyes revealed. After another fleeting smile, she flung
open the door to her world.

The spare bedroom was draped in white sheets, shielding furniture and whatnot. Four easels occupied the
center, forming a semicircle with displayed canvasses in
various stages. A group of completed works off to our
immediate left were purposely arranged in a row beside
stacks of frames. The woman had a damned assembly
line, engaging in a chase of whatever fleeting memories or phantoms besieged her. A paintbrush rested in a
bamboo brush holder beside a tray of paints, which she
picked up to return to work on the canvass furthest to
our right.

"Ever been to the Netherlands, Chase? I call this one
Happiness," Ava stated as she painted what appeared to
be the rough beginnings of a red lighthouse above a rocky

cliff. Strange sailboats, similar to that in others paintings I recalled from my online research on her, drifted lazily below. But it was hard to concentrate on the art though, due to the artist, animalistic urges and all. "It's too simplistic a name, though," she said, continuing her monologue. "I'm sure they'll ask me to change it."

"Is that the setting for this painting? The Netherlands?" I asked, walking up behind her, needing to be in her proximity. I slowly touched her hair, letting my fingers gently comb through the ends before resting them on her shoulder. There was a brief moment when her hips bumped into my pelvis, to which I closed my eyes, thinking of better things I could be doing with her.

"I was in a bad way when I came here," she said, ignoring my question as well as my hand and abruptly leaving an untold story to herself. "Smith befriended me. Helped me adapt and get established. Found this place for me too."

"Did he pay for it?" I asked brusquely, having seen such things before. I wasn't naive to the wants and desires of older, wealthy men in this city or any other, for that matter.

"Yes, he did," she replied. "I had nothing."

"Oh," I offered, moving my hand away. The distance between our bodies widened.

"Don't be jealous, Chase. He's gay," Ava said, giggling, as she turned to dab the tip of my nose with her brush. "You're more of his type. But he knows you're off-limits."

"If he didn't, I'd sure set him straight."

Ava chuckled. "Straight. Unintended pun, huh? Don't be such a homophobe, Chase."

"I'm not a homophobe."

"Yes, you are. I remember that time when we were in—" She stopped, closing her eyes as she mumbled something to herself too low to make out.

"There you go again. Stop it," I chided.

"What?" she said, feigning innocence as she turned in the middle of a brush stroke. I knocked the paintbrush from her hand, a rage built upon a foundation of frustration consuming me. It fell onto the drop cloth beneath our feet. I grasped her shoulders, backing her against the wall. I moved closer to where our breath intermingled.

"I'm tired of these little things where I'm lost as to what you're talking about, Ava. And it has to stop. Who are you? And how do you know so much about me?"

"I know you like any good wife should," she said, her lips forming a smile before she licked them for my benefit. Still toying with me. I released my grip on her, regretting my outburst.

"Stop. Stop saying stuff like that. You're not my wife. You turn me on, and you know you do, but other times you make me nervous . . . scared. This is one of those times. Stop fucking with me, Ava."

"Do you think I'm just toying with you?"

"Maybe. Because this—this doesn't make sense, despite our mutual attraction. It's crazy. I can't get you out my head. And I must be out my ever-loving mind," I said, nervously rotating the wedding band on my finger a half turn with my thumb.

"Do you think I'm crazy, Chase?"

"No. But I don't understand you. And I need to. Help me make sense of this."

"What if you didn't believe what I told you? And it drove you away?"

"It couldn't. Unless you used to be a man," I joked. "Does this Smith dude understand you?"

Ava gulped. "Yes," she replied.

"What makes him so special?"

"I didn't risk anything by telling him everything about

me. I don't love him, Chase. Not like that, at least. And despite all the help he's been, it would hurt, but I could afford to lose him. I can't lose you. Not now. Not again."

"*Again?*"

"I mean . . . when you left the other day," she said, picking up her paintbrush off the floor. She gracefully placed it back on the tray next to her paints. "I wanted to stay in your arms and never leave the bed. Wanted to hear you say my name softly from your weary lips long into the night. But I knew you had to go."

"'Yeah. I had to. I have a wife. A life . . . beyond this."

"Even if it's the wrong life?"

"Don't say that. You don't know me well enough to say something like that. I think I better go. I have work to do back at the office. They're probably looking for me."

"Even if you could be doing something else? Something better with your life?"

"Now you're sounding like my wife. She's always getting on me about not finishing law school."

"I wasn't referring to law school . . . or that office where you work. It's nice, beautiful even, but you could share so much more of yourself with the world."

I chuckled, eyeing my watch. Should've been back to work over an hour ago. No one would say anything, but I had a pile of work waiting on me. Instead, I was behaving like a flighty schoolkid at a fast-food joint with a ton of options. "What are you getting at?" I asked.

"Entertain me for just a moment longer. Look under that sheet in the corner," she said, pointing at a large, bulky covered object.

I knew what it was the moment I came closer. Could make out the outline before my fingers pinched the white sheet and tugged. A piano.

"Nice," I said with a smile, dragging my fingers across the keys. "But I don't play anymore."

"Try, Chase. For me."

"Was this your husband's?"

"No. But he had one similar to that."

"And you want me to help you relive memories? Memories of him?"

"No. I want you to create your own memories. Pursue your own dreams."

"This . . . this isn't my dream," I snapped, reflecting on a time long ago. "You've got me wrong. All wrong."

I stormed away from the piano, annoyed with whatever type of manipulation she was attempting. Ava hastily moved into my path, barring me from a quick exit.

"Chase, don't be mad at me. That wasn't my intent," she said, resting the palms of her hands on my chest.

"What are you trying to do, then? You keep saying things that don't make sense, but then you know more about me than my wife. Little things that nobody knows. You say you know me from college, but I know you don't. You couldn't. You do things to me that if I knew you back then . . . Well."

"I—I'm sorry to be putting you through this, Chase. And I want to be honest with you."

"Then tell me how you really know me, damn it!"

"Because you're my husband, Chase! You're my husband! We met in college and we were married! Happily married! Not you and this other woman! Then . . . you left me. You died."

What she said didn't make a lick of sense, but staring into her eyes . . .

She believed it.

18

She's crazy. Has to be, I thought to myself. I'd left Ava there as she tried explaining herself fully. But I refused to listen further. I couldn't hear anymore lest I got dragged into her delusional world.

Now, a full twenty-four hours later, I couldn't escape her voice.

The jury of twelve watched and waited, wondering what Jim Warner, the senior partner, fumbled for at our table after abruptly halting his diatribe. Our client Iris kept her head low, despite Jim's impromptu coaching, refusing to look toward the jury stand.

"Chase, where are Jacobi's notes on exhibit number five?" Jim asked in a low voice, expressing his displeasure with trying this matter on such short notice. Jacobi had called in sick this morning, bailing on Iris's case after things went south. The black eye he received last night from her husband over a *misunderstanding* wasn't going to be brought up by me. But still, his carelessness didn't reflect well on the firm—something Jim Warner was sure to consider when debating over accepting Jacobi as partner with them.

"I don't know, Jim" I answered absently, not meaning to say what I thought as I fished around the stacks of trial material on our table. I could be careless too, my mind addled from too many restless nights.

My first night after leaving Ava, I'd dreamed of the Netherlands, somewhere I'd never been. The red lighthouse in her painting was as real as the waking world. I stood impatiently before it while she maneuvered me with her hand for the perfect camera shot. And I was happy, smiling at her contently while heeding her directions. Waiting for a flash while fixated on a row of slowly spinning windmills behind her in the distance, separated from us by fields of tulips as far as the eye could see. At peace while those odd sailboats drifted in the choppy waters offshore. Great. Living in someone else's dream. She'd successfully pulled me past the event horizon of her maddening world, the gravity of her false beliefs offering no chance at escape.

A loud harrumph snapped me back to my reality. Jim clearing his throat as a stalling tactic.

"Get it together, Chase. You're about as useful today as a one-legged man in an ass-kicking contest," he caustically remarked under his breath before turning to face the judge. "Your Honor, may I approach the bench?" he asked in his turned-up small-town drawl. Judge Kemp covered his microphone to let out a deep sigh before motioning both attorneys to approach the bench. Then he instructed the jury to be patient, explaining that the legal process wasn't always smooth and organized, but prone to fits and starts.

As the mustached judge spoke in whispered tones to both Jim and the lead defense attorney, I checked my watch. Despite our less-than-stellar start, this trial might be salvaged due to the time at hand. It was close enough to lunchtime that the jury had become impatient. Perfect opportunity for the judge to set them free so they could return focused. And it would give Jim time enough to retrieve the absent trial materials from Jacobi's possession and consult with him.

The lunch break would also do Iris well, as she was probably spent and flustered from last night's circus.

Once the jury was excused for lunch, Jim immediately turned to me.

"Want me to track down, Jacobi?" I asked, ready to do the damage control I'd done so many times in the past to cover my friend's ass.

"No. I'll speak with Mr. Stewart. Don't you worry about that," Jim replied. "Our client looks like she needs some fresh air. Why don't you mind her? I trust there won't be any complications from a married man such as yourself."

"No. Not at all," was all I could say about being volunteered by Jim to baby-sit. After all, he paid my check. I was guaranteed not to be a problem like Jacobi, but Jim might feel otherwise if he knew my current dilemma.

"Ready to get out of here and take a break?" I asked cheerfully, offering my hand for the deathly quiet Iris to take. I said nothing further, leaving it to her if she'd respond. On our way out the courtroom, I sent a quick text to Jacobi.

Jim's looking 4 u. Pissed. Not good, bro.

I led Iris outside the courthouse, skipping the basement cafeteria's fair for some good Southern cooking, a ritual I tried to follow whenever my schedule permitted. We crossed a traffic-lined Fannin Street and walked the two blocks up Congress past a closed Red Cat Jazz Café, frequented by me and Dawn on Sundays. Making a quick left on Travis, we arrived at Treebeard's restaurant, housed inside the Baker-Travis Building, the second oldest building in Houston.

The sullen Latina, still playing mute, cracked a smile when the smell of fresh cooking hit her nose. Probably hadn't eaten much nor thought about food since last night. Not sure of what she wanted to order, she motioned for me to go ahead. I was salivating for my usual: the red beans and rice with sausage along with a slice of their homemade jalapeño cornbread. I looked back to see Iris's decision, a lone bowl of shrimp étouffée and a can of diet Dr Pepper, on her tray.

"That's it? Have you had their butter cake?" I asked her as I slid my tray along toward the cashier. She needed her energy up for the afternoon session.

"No," she solemnly replied. It must have taken all of her strength to come downtown and sit through a trial with neither support from her husband nor Jacobi. After putting our meals on the company credit card, I found an open table for us amid the other lunch patrons. We parked ourselves outside beneath the ceiling fans, facing the bit of green space across the street that is Market Square. The sparse decor, aged architecture, and balcony above reminded me of a time when we might've been greeted by horse-drawn carriages on Travis Street rather than cars and bicycles.

"How do you think the case is going?" I asked, engaging in more small talk to crack her shell.

"That man Jim. He hates me," she replied, moving her straight ebony hair away from her pleasant yet weary face. For the first time today, she made eye contact. Progress.

"Naww," I scoffed. "He's just focused on your case. Once this is over, he'll loosen up. Trust me." Jim didn't hate Iris. I doubt he cared about her one way or the other. He just hated the mess this case had devolved into thanks to Jacobi's inability to keep his dick in his pants. I said nothing about her husband's attack on Jacobi, having caught them slipping at Hotel Zaza last night when he recognized her car and decided to follow. Remained noncommittal despite what she assumed.

"Have you talked to Charla lately?" she asked, referring to Ava by her artist pseudonym.

"Not since that day at the Breakfast Klub," I replied, unsure if Iris was another one of those patrons of Ava, like Smith Sampson. Still, my business was my own.

"There's no need to lie to me. I would be the last one to talk. People in glass houses and all," she said, motioning toward my wedding band.

I chuckled nervously, taking a moment to look at my phone and the series of recent messages from Ava to which I hadn't replied. "Maybe once since then," I responded. "How long you known her?"

"We met a few years ago. By chance. Jacobi told you what I said?"

"About sharing the same therapist? Yes."

Iris's lips tightened. "Yeah. Jacobi talks too much. I'm not one to strike up conversations with fellow patients, but we shared the elevator once . . . and she just seemed so approachable."

"Relax. There's nothing wrong with that."

"What if it comes up in trial?"

"You're not alone when it comes to those needing a little help in coping with the pressures of life. At least you sought it. If they ask you about it, just tell the truth. If they get too belligerent, Jim will step in. Our firm is the best at what we do, Mrs. Wilson."

She chuckled. "Funny hearing you say my married name. After all these years I'd finally gotten used to it. Used to hyphenate like crazy."

"What's your maiden name?"

"Garcia," she answered haughtily. "I certainly don't look like a Wilson, eh?"

"You said it. Not me," I said with a grin, noticing the innate sex appeal Jacobi had acted upon recklessly.

"What's your last name, Chase?"

"Hidalgo."

"You're Latino?"

"My dad," I answered, wobbling my hand for effect to show that was only half my heritage. "*Cubano.*"

"Oooh. Do you speak—"

"Not in the least," I said, cutting her off with a wave of the same hand. I cut into my sausage link and quickly stabbed the loose piece with my fork. "My dad wasn't around to teach me much of anything, let alone Spanish. Musician 'n all."

"Is he famous?"

"Used to be," I said with a grimace. I'd broken the ice and got her mind off stuff, now it was twenty questions with me on the receiving end. "Performed with a band called the Asylum Seekers decades ago."

"Wait. Hidalgo. Joell Hidalgo? *Nooo.* Joell Hidalgo's your father?"

"Yeah. That's him."

"Wow. My father used to listen to them when I was a kid. I used to dance along with him. He was a photographer for one of the old music rags. Told me he saw your papi and the Asylum Seekers in concert down in Miami when they were just getting started. He left me one of their albums—*Follow Me, No?* Good old vinyl. Do you play an instrument as well? Hell, music's in your blood. You have to."

"No. Not at all. Are you doing okay after last night?" I asked, deftly turning the conversation back to her despite my reluctance to throw her blowup in her face. She left me no choice.

"Yes. I'm fine, considering. What did Jacobi tell you?"

"Just the bare minimum. Let me know he needed someone at the firm to fill in for him. I don't have a law license, so that is where Jim comes in."

"You strike me as very capable. Maybe more so than your friend," Iris admitted. "Why aren't you a lawyer?"

"Go figure," I said deadpan. I was getting tired of people focusing on my career choices. Like I was some

kind of poster child for missed opportunities. "Is everything going to be okay for you at home? Your husband
didn't lay his hands on you, did he?"

"No. For that, I'm lucky. We have children and I fucked
up, Mr. Hidalgo. Who knows, maybe your firm will have
another case of mine—a divorce. Think that man Jim
would like me then? This whole thing is so embarrass-
ing. Can't believe I let myself get caught up."

"I can kinda empathize with that; getting caught up
in something."

Iris got a glint in her eye. Another diversion from
her troubles. "Charla. She's a lovely woman. Inside and
out. I'm not surprised she appeals to you."

"Charla. Do you always call her that?" I probed.

"Yes. But I don't know if she knows me by Iris. Confidentiality," she chuckled. Color returned to her face.

"How well do you know her?"

"Why?"

"Because. I'm curious."

"What do you want to know?"

I looked at my watch. We still had a few minutes to
spare before hurrying back to the courthouse. Iris began to speak, hopefully illuminating my understanding
of Ava and her wild ideas. I moved my empty plate to
the side, leaning closer to hear what she had to say.

But her mouth froze at the first syllable, her lip quivering instead of speaking further. Her neck craned to
allow her to better see something over my shoulder.

"What's wrong?" I asked.

The rev of a truck engine drowned out my voice. I turned
to see a large Ford F250 diesel pickup as it lurched forward.
It jumped the curb, partially rolling onto the sidewalk near
our table and almost striking a support column. I leaped
from my seat, fearful of being run over. But it stopped short,
the truck door swinging open as its driver stepped out.

"Another one, Iris? How many more are there?" the tall white man yelled, his voice cracking from the strain. He wore a Texas A&M baseball cap, a pair of basic blue jeans—probably Wranglers—but the tan button-down and light leather jacket spoke of an engineer or some kind of problem solver who preferred getting out in the field rather than being tied to a desk. Iris's husband, I presumed, without much thought.

"Honey. No. He works for the law firm. My—my trial. We're just having lunch," Iris urged with her outstretched hands trembling.

"Like hell you are! Lunch? Like dinner last night with that n—"

"Sir, please calm down," I said quickly, before the disparaging word I assumed was about to come out his mouth could be said. "I can assure you nothing inappropriate is going on. My name is Chase Hidalgo with—" I said just as her husband charged me, blind and deaf to reason.

19

I sat like some scolded schoolkid, pouting in the principal's office for the past half hour. Ignoring my bruised and tender knuckles, I reviewed the recent message on my phone.

Chase. I'm not crazy. Miss u. Pls call.

I didn't need to be reading this at the moment. I quickly deleted Ava's message and stowed my phone. Most of the staff at Casey, Warner & Associates had gone home for the evening. The only thing breaking the silence was the clicking of the brass clock on the wall. Finally, the door cracked. I stood up, straightening my shirt and tie before I entered the conference room. I caught the faint trailing murmurs of brief conversations hastily ending the closer I got.

They sat around the splendid executive table, silently judging everything from my body language to my facial expression. As if they didn't truly know me before. Friends and colleagues most times, but not tonight. Jim Warner, Abner Casey, Maryann Milner, and Rick Stein—the senior partners of Casey, Warner & Associates—were hastily gathered to do damage control and protect their necks. My frayed nerves and total frustration were bubbling over. Had me wanting to throw up.

"Do you know what you did, Chase?" Rick Stein asked, breaking the silence with his high-pitched voice as I sat down at the closest open seat. He had the most cordial relationship with me, so they'd probably delegated this to him after Jim Warner brought them up to speed on everything. As Jim sat stonefaced, his eyes spoke of sheer disappointment when I looked into them.

"Yes," I answered softly, having decided on my answer while fretting over their deliberations beyond these doors. "I beat his ass."

"Excuse me?" Maryann Milner sputtered, obviously flabbergasted. She was already planning another run for district judge in the upcoming elections. I turned my eyes to her.

"I beat his ass," I answered again, worn and tired over my shabby treatment by everyone, starting with Jacobi for crashing this ship on the proverbial rocks. Iris's enraged husband was wrong for attacking me at Treebeard's, but I escalated matters by not turning the other cheek. Maybe I could've sloughed him off like a minor annoyance and eased up after my first punch put him on his ass. But I didn't. I refused to relent, instead raining down several more until Iris begged me to stop. Like I said, I was on a short fuse with little sleep. Perhaps he gave me a chance to vent my frustrations. Frustrations over that damn woman Ava and how she was making me look at things. Frustrations over doing the same stuff everyday that I really didn't want to do. But did it with a smile and maximum effort anyway. Playing the good little worker bee because that's what was expected of me. Good old dependable Chase.

Playing.

The same old song. Day in and day out.

Rather than coming up with a new tune.

Maybe the smile and certainty was a course I could no longer maintain.

"Chase," Jim Warner interrupted, sensing it was his turn to add something. He continued, "We don't 'beat asses' at Casey Warner. At least not on the street. Only in court, son. What was a good malpractice case has de-volved into an embarrassment—a dad-gum three-ring circus—due to the actions of Jacobi and you."

"Me? But I—"

"Yes, son. Nobody else did that to our client's hus-band's face outside Treebeard's."

"And nobody told him to lay his hands on me, Jim," I responded, my blood pressure rising.

"Which he wouldn't have if not for some alleged im-proprieties with his wife. And from what I understand, Mrs. Wilson had to pull you off him. Do you have any-thing else to say? Besides the obligatory bravado you're displaying?"

I sighed. "No. I put up with a lot of stuff for all of you . . . for the betterment of this firm. Things above and beyond what I am paid to do. And I'm damn good at it. I don't think anything else needs to be said."

"And I agree with your assessment, Chase," Abner Casey, the elder statesman who was rarely seen these days, added. "We know you're an asset to this firm. However, this isn't about what you've done day in and day out. This is about what you did today. And what you did was wrong."

"Chase, we talked things over after Jim informed us of today's events," Rick Stein said, asserting himself as the lead voice once again. "We've decided that you should take some time off. Cool off while we try to sort this out and figure out how best to deal with Mrs. Wil-son, her husband's potential civil suit, and the expo-sure to our firm."

As I stormed out of the office, I don't know which was greater at the moment: My embarrassment over having to share this news with Dawn. Or my insane de-sire to be with Ava.

Parked on the corner of Oak Place and Baldwin Street,

outside the Midtown Arbor Place apartments, I learned the answer to that unbalanced equation.

I dialed home.

"How's the trial going, babe?" Dawn asked, stifling a yawn.

"Not so good. A bunch of unexpected developments threw everything into turmoil here at the firm. Shit's really hit the fan," I said, withholding the nature of the shit.

"Want to talk about it?"

"Can't. Confidentiality."

"Okay," she said, followed by a pregnant pause. "When are you coming home?"

"It'll be way late. A ton of damage control to do. All the partners are over here. Expected to put in overtime tonight," I said, focusing on my wedding band as it glistened in the streetlight. I closed my eyes and swallowed hard. "Get some sleep."

"Mmm. Okay. Love you, babe."

"Love you too," I replied, tasting the hollowness of it.

Need 2 C U. Despite . . .

I texted Ava after hanging up with Dawn.

K. When?

Soon.

It would be another full ten minutes before I exited my car, seeking *something*.

Not some further explanation for Ava's delusions. Just the unexplainable I felt when I was with her.

"I can't keep coming back," I said aloud, as if a junkie at the threshold of a crackhouse.

"And yet here you are," Ava said softly.

20

Must've been at least three in the morning. I stretched, then slowly rose, careful not to disturb Ava with whom I'd been spooning prior to giving in to deep slumber. I refused to discuss her delusions any further lest she scare me away as before. But I convinced myself that I could help her . . . somehow. Not sure if making love to her again would be considered useful, but I was weak. Weakened by her beauty and the unusual, thrilling magnetism that existed between us. Partially true. It was fascinating that she knew me so well. Something I should've analyzed and observed from a distance. Clinical. Like I'd learned in law school, before giving up on that path. But I had to be closer. Needed to immerse myself in Ava on so many levels. One of them that took us to this moment : . . again. Sin and sustenance interwoven where knowing wasn't as important as simply *being*. Shit. She had me wanting to believe her. Believe in her. Maybe insanity was contagious.

As I rose from the bed, I found my watch on the floor atop my shirt. The damned woman didn't believe in clocks around here. Of course, if time did stand still in this room, I wouldn't be in so much trouble right about now.

I strained my eyes to read the tiny dial hands by the dim light. I was lucky. It was closer to 1:30.

Ava mumbled. Called out my name before succumbing again to her sex-induced coma. Felt natural. Like she had been with me more years than weeks. But I wasn't her husband. Ever. Catching my bearings, I shuffled toward her bathroom. Beneath the refreshing waters of the showerhead, I had a moment of clarity free of Ava's influence. I slapped my forehead, suddenly feeling regret over the beatdown I'd administered Iris's husband. Then the deeper regret of what I'd been doing to my own wife Dawn raked at my stomach. Sighing, I reached for the bar of soap, working up a vigorous lather on the washcloth so I could scour Ava's DNA off my body. But that would only work so well. She was beneath my skin and, dare I say it, close to my heart and not just my dick.

Moments later I toweled off, looking at my weary face in the mirror of the medicine cabinet. I saw the face of a liar and cheat staring back. A stranger to me. Maybe Dawn was right; maybe I was supposed to be a lawyer. Something told me to me reach out. Rather than touching reversed palms with my doppelganger, I grasped the edges of the mirror and pulled it toward me. It came open with a click, exposing the medicine cabinet behind it. I quickly scanned for the familiar brown of a prescription bottle. There were two situated in the bottom right corner. I paused, listening for any activity in the bedroom. Without further hesitation, I grabbed both of them, quickly scanning the labels. One was a two-year-old bottle for Xanax and one a little newer for Depakote. From the dates, I assumed Ava was no longer taking either one. Maybe explaining her fascination with me, but not her familiarity. The prescribing doctor was a Charla Prisbani. I chuckled, seeing the irony of Ava's pseudonym now—taking her doctor's first name. I surmised the Nuttier part was a bit of wit from being accused of being *nuttier than a fruitcake*. Wonderful. Now I was seeing into her head. I carefully placed the prescription bottles back where I'd found them, leaving my reflection in the mirror to wonder what I was up to.

I eased back into the bedroom, determined to creep out on her. Parting was difficult enough already. I hastily donned my underwear and slacks, grabbing my shirt and accessories to put on as I made my way out. In the hallway, I could've easily made it to the front door.

If not for that damn room of Ava's.

I took another look at my watch, knowing further delays wouldn't be beneficial to my health. Ignoring common sense once again, I pushed open the door to her escape space. The painting of the lighthouse was completed. Looked ready for another sale or exhibit. She'd begun another one. This time it was of a mirror—funny considering my medicine-cabinet encounter—with a woman's hand touching it. The image in the mirror wasn't completed just yet, only a bare outline of whatever was being reflected. Left me curious for the finished product. Moving on with my attention, I saw the throw still remained off the piano in the corner. Probably just the way it had been left the last time I was here.

Alone, I took time to admire it. It was a fine, sturdy baby grand. Reminded me of the one played for shoppers at Nordstrom in the Galleria. Wondered how difficult it was for the movers to get it inside this space.

I took a seat, perching my fingers lightly atop the keys. I took a deep breath, imagining I was in a concert hall before an attentive audience.

"It's calling to you," Ava said, making me almost jump to the ceiling with surprise. I hated being startled. She'd donned a silk robe, short and the color of a soft rose. A gentle smile graced her face after she completed her yawn. "When I didn't hear the door alarm, I knew you'd be in here."

"Was about to go. Didn't want to wake you."

"Guilt kicking in again?" Ava asked, gliding closer on those firm legs of her. The robe outlined then relinquished the lines of her body with each step.

"Perhaps," I replied.

"Going to play it for me this time, Chase?"

"No. I can't," I said, thinking back to a time as a young boy, when I got my first true impression of my father, the oh-so-great music man. And vowed to never follow in his footsteps.

Ava took a seat, scrunching next to me on the padded piano bench. "Just try," she said, resting her head on my shoulder. "I know you can," she offered as she softly rubbed my forearm. I took a deep breath, closed my eyes, and allowed my instincts to guide me. I began to play by ear, just as I'd learned, doing the opening piano riff to Tupac's "I Ain't Mad Atcha" as a joke.

I stopped, looking at Ava as she righted her head. "Y'know . . . Pac," I said with a chuckle.

Ava's brow crinkled in the dark. I waited a moment longer.

"Tupac. 'I Ain't Mad Atcha.' From his album *All Eyez On Me*. You don't listen to rap, huh?"

"Ohhh," she said absentmindedly. "Tupac. I'm a little slow. From *before* he became mayor of Oakland."

"Mayor of Oakland? Cute," I said with a smile as I raised a skeptical eyebrow at her. "Pac's dead. Unless you're one of those conspiracy buffs."

"Me? No. I must be thinking about someone else."

"You are the odd one," I said, grasping her hand and kissing it. "Always looking at things in unusual ways, like what *might've been*. You see the potential in all of us, I guess."

"You would see the potential too if you stayed with me, Chase. I promise."

"You know I can't."

"Do you love me, Chase?"

"I—"

"Spare me. I can say it freely. I love you, Mr. Chase Hidalgo."

I abruptly stood up, feeling that turn in the air when things get weird. Thought about those old prescriptions in the medicine cabinet. I'd been enabling her. Pure selfishness. "Ava, I've seen how things can get. Especially today," I said as I reflected on Iris. "Today I beat up a man, probably more out of guilt than necessity. And I don't want my wife feeling like the man I beat up. I'm sorry to be adding to your confusion every time I come around. That's why you won't be seeing me anymore."

Maybe she sensed the difference in my tone, the resolve I was trying to project. As I crossed my leg over the piano bench to leave, Ava rushed to stand up as well. We collided. Off balance, I fell to the floor.

"No! You can't leave me!" she said, her robe coming undone as she bent over to either assist me up or barricade my exit. I looked away, avoiding staring at her lovely body. I wanted nothing more than to be reckless a while longer and take her once again. To slide up inside her on this floor and feel her tremble and writhe beneath me in ecstasy. As she came closer, I braced my arm.

"Back up. Please," I said, firmly yet minus any animosity.

"You don't mean it. Here, let me help you up," she said, her proximity threatening to erode my will.

"No. I said, 'back up', Ava. I have to go."

No real surprise, she ignored me. Ava grasped me as I stood up, hugging me tight and refusing to let go. We tussled as I forcibly pried her arms from around me. In my haste, I accidentally knocked her into her the easel. The easel fell sideways, catapulting her newest project across the room, where it bounced off a wall. The crash of her work gave both of us pause. In that moment, I looked into Ava's eyes and saw something beyond sadness. I saw a dark desperation that frightened me. And that moment, I knew this had to be over.

"This isn't how it was supposed to be," Ava said, looking suddenly defeated. I was still breathing heavily as I rushed past her. She dropped to her knees, moving her hair out of her face as tears ran uncontrollably down her face.

"I'm not sure about that, but know it never should have been. I was wrong to lead you on," I offered, briefly pausing in the doorway. "I apologize for this trouble and wish you well."

"You don't love her! I'll make it right, Chase! I'll make it right," she yelled, leaving me more than a little concerned as I closed the front door behind me.

21

I reached my hand from under the comforter, fishing for my iPhone until I found it. I checked the number before answering.

"Where are you?" Dawn asked before I could even say hello, disturbing me from the briefest bit of escape. Took a moment for me to realize where I was. I sat up, seeing the crumpled bag from Frenchy's chicken on the desk along with two empty Heineken bottles. After driving around mindlessly, I'd grabbed some food and checked into Hotel Derek on Westheimer near the Galleria. Going home would've been unseemly after what had happened with Ava.

"Jacobi's," I answered. "We were up so late that I didn't want to disturb you. Was also too lazy to make the drive."

"Uh-huh. And how many drinks did you have?"

"A few," I replied with a chuckle.

"Good of you not to drive, then. Still missed you, though."

"Ditto," I said.

"Chase, this house is lonely with you working late all the time. We need to think about filling that spare bedroom."

"I thought you were more concerned with me being a lawyer," I chirped, regretting it almost immediately as it left my lips.

"I haven't forgotten about that. But I'm not getting any younger. And no one said we couldn't multitask."

Since turning thirty, Dawn's maternal desires had come to the fore.

"Okay. We'll talk," I said. "Right now, I'm about to get up and hit it, babe. I'll see you when I get off. Leaving early today. Maybe we can 'multitask' then."

But I didn't have work to go into. Not with the senior partners having put me on involuntary leave.

I rolled over, deleting the new texts from Ava, then completely removing her number from my phone. Damn sunlight coming through the window was bothersome. I placed one of my pillows over my head then went back to sleep. The world could wait a while longer.

Eventually I moved from the bed, placing a call down to the concierge for some last-minute dry-cleaning. Looking semi-crisp yet again, I checked out around 3:00 P.M., figuring it was time to go home.

As I turned into my neighborhood, I received a call from my prodigal friend.

"Bro, I'm so sorry for not calling you back. You at the office?"

"No. I'm driving home. Not going to be at the office for the near future. They sent me home yesterday for laying hands excessively on Iris's husband. She didn't tell you?"

"No, man. I haven't talked to her since he dotted my eye. Figured it best. Thanks for hemming him up for me, bruh."

"It wasn't for you, man. He just came along at the wrong time. And it wouldn't have happened if you hadn't mixed business with pleasure. Dude, you dumped a lot of shit on the firm. And this 'hiding out' hasn't helped matters. You need to grow the fuck up," I said, getting it off my chest.

"Okay! I got it, Chase. I'ma get my head out my ass. And I'm sorry about you getting caught up in my shit. I'll make it right. I promise."

"I'll believe it when I'm back to work," I said tersely, hanging up as I arrived home, prepared to pretend the last twenty-four hours hadn't happened. *For the sake of my marriage*, I thought to myself.

Entering my home from the garage, I was greeted by sounds of conversation. Dawn had company, so I quickly composed myself.

"There's my baby," my mom said as I came around the corner. She and Dawn were gathered in the kitchen over a pot of chili on the stove. Never good with two chefs in charge, but they seemed to be making do. I put on my best smile, set down my briefcase, and gave my mom a kiss.

"Can't believe someone got you out your house," I teased her as I wrapped my arms around my wife.

"I volunteered to take your mother grocery shopping since you've been swamped with your big trial," Dawn volunteered as she rubbed my back. "And since I'm off tomorrow, I begged her to have dinner and stay the night."

"That was so sweet of you," I said as I kissed her on the lips. Right when I'd become this stranger in our marriage, Dawn was doing all the right things.

"How was your day, baby?" Dawn asked.

"Less hectic than yesterday," I replied, glad that my knuckles barely showed wear from what I'd done at Treebeard's. My phone buzzed, interrupting my response. I quickly checked it to see if it was Ava. Despite my deleting her number, I'd memorized it. I ignored the call, but it did succeed in bringing my pressing issues to the forefront.

"Baby, been meaning to surprise you with something. And now is as good a time as any."

"Oh?" Dawn said, taking a quick stir of her chili. Her face lit up from the suspense.

"Both of us have been so busy. I think we need some

time together for just us. Kind of like what you were hinting at this morning." Dawn smiled even more. "Let's take a cruise, baby. This week. We can sail out of Galveston . . . spend a week in faraway lands. The seas, the sun, a little sand. What do ya say?"

My mom had a curious look on her face. A look I intentionally ignored, but couldn't help but notice. She'd probably heard similar slick proposals from my dad. When I turned my focus back to Dawn, she had dropped the gleeful smile. Her hands now rested on her hips.

"Baby, you mentioned a cruise before. Remember? You know I can't with my work. And how can you take that kind of time off with your ongoing big case? You know Jacobi doesn't know what he's doing."

"Dawn, let's not get into that. I—no—*we* deserve some time off. Forget my job and your job. Let's do this. We can begin packing tomorrow."

"Maybe another time, Chase. I'll have to check my schedule at Macy's. Besides, we can't go this week anyway. We have an art exhibit to attend."

"Excuse me? What art exhibit?" I asked, trying to fathom what she was talking about. Maybe I'd been so preoccupied that something had slipped my mind.

Dawn smiled coyly. "Remember that woman?" she asked.

"No," I replied, trying to hide how perturbed I was. "*Who?*"

"Charla Nuttier." My throat tightened as my mind tried to interpret anything beyond the two words she'd just strung together. Despite trying to hide it, I looked at my wife like she was plumb crazy.

"Dawn, what do you mean?"

"Me and your mom ran into her at the new HEB supermarket over on FM 2920 and Spring Cypress Road . . . of all places. We were grocery shopping and the woman struck up a casual conversation while we were in line at checkout. Then I find out she's the same artist you had pulled up online that time. Small world, huh?"

"Crazy," I mumbled. The small world felt more like a broom closet right about now. What was Ava up to? No way it was a coincidence.

"I know. And she's *sooo* beautiful in person. Anyway, she invited us to her next showing. This week! Can you believe it? Her card is on the counter over there," she said, motioning with one hand while tasting the chili from her spoon. My mom walked over to the cabinet to get some bowls for us.

"And you really want to go?" I asked timidly.

"Certainly!" Dawn gushed as she added another shake of chili powder to the pot, then stirred again.

"I might have to work," I said, fumbling for words. I still stood in the center of the kitchen. My mom moved past me to retrieve silverware from the drawer to my right, probably wondering why I hadn't moved aside.

"But you mentioned the cruise like you had the time already set aside. Chase . . . is something the matter?" Dawn asked as both she and my mom eyed me suspiciously. Now, neither one of them was moving. My legs felt weighted down with lead.

Again my phone buzzed. I wanted to hurl it and watch it smash into a million pieces.

22

"You sure you don't feel like going home. Maybe work on dessert?" I teased as we edged toward the hustling valet attendant, several cars ahead. Under any other circumstances, I would welcome this evening with my wife. But tonight, I couldn't even enjoy the new car smell of the Acura I'd bought just days earlier; my mind stressing over what the evening might have in store. We'd had dinner at Gravitas around the corner on Taft prior to coming here—Ava's exhibit at the Stuart & Graf art gallery on Rhode Place off Allen Parkway and Buffalo Bayou. If I'd been smart, I'd have picked a restaurant way in Katy and counted on traffic to snarl en route. But perhaps I was as anxious to see the artist as was my wife. Sometimes destruction came in appealing packages.

"No. And thank you for dinner, sweetheart. I really want to see those paintings up close. It's not every day you receive a personal invite from an artist. Besides, we'll have time to work on dessert afterward," Dawn replied, grasping the top of my hand as it rested on the gearshift. I'd just bought the TSX to replace the Camry I'd wrecked. Had to keep with the pretense that I was gainfully employed while still waiting for Jacobi to go to bat for me. Thanks to Dawn's work schedule, at least I was able to stay home most of this week without pretending to go in. She'd never questioned how I made it home ahead of her each day.

I became impatient as we came closer. The red brick

building seemed to radiate menace despite the joyful looks on people's faces as they exited their cars and entered. "Could've parked myself," I muttered.

"You're just as excited as me. I knew it," Dawn said smugly. If only she knew. Really.

"Not excited about the crowd."

"It is crowded," she said agreeing with me. "We really hit the big ticket in town tonight, huh?"

I didn't respond. My mind was elsewhere. I considered letting Dawn come alone, but couldn't risk it. If Ava sought her out like that in a grocery store, she probably knew where we lived and had followed Dawn. And who knew Ava's true intentions, except that she was challenging me.

She wanted me to confront her, to go to her. Back into her arms where maybe she'd ensnare me in her fantasy world for good.

I'd meant it when I ended things with Ava, going so far as to change my phone number, but here I was. I had to know what she really wanted with my wife and be there to save my marriage, if it came to that, from the threat of someone who knew me better than the lovely woman in the passenger seat beside me. Despite it making no sense, someone had to have fed Ava such intimate information about me because the alternative made even less sense.

Earlier in the day, I'd gambled on strength in numbers, asking my mom to come with us. But she declined, mumbling something about *bougie stuff* not being her cup of tea. I think, being a mother, she sensed a storm brewing on the waters and figured it best to ride it out safely ashore. She did share that something about this "Charla Nuttier art woman" unnerved her when they met at HEB. As if by the look in her eye and the way she smiled, the art woman was privy to an inside joke. Reminded my mom of some of the women she'd crossed paths with in dealing with my dad all those years gone by. That comment alone was enough to rattle me all through dinner with Dawn. If my mom had picked up on that, was Dawn far behind?

Our car doors were opened for us upon pulling up. One valet helped Dawn out by her hand, welcoming her to the art gallery in as cordial a manner as possible without being over the top. Mine silently, efficiently handed me my claim ticket and cracked a minimal smile before jumping into my driver's seat to speed off.

I briefly brushed off my black jacket to remove any crumbs from dinner, then took Dawn's arm to escort her inside. I watched her as she did a quick tease of her short brown tresses and sighed mildly. Not from stress, as had been my constant companion, but from joy. Shedding her more conservative work attire, my wife was amazingly put together—a dash of colorful fabric, lovely brown skin tone, and fine body that I didn't appreciate enough, scooped up inside a buttercup strapless silk dress. She was delicate and poised, yet seductive. And with a Macy's discount that came in handy.

"You're looking very handsome tonight, Chase. Maybe we can set aside a weekly date night."

Kissing her hand, I replied, "I'd like that, babe."

From the mumblings, it seemed nobody expected this kind of turnout. Guests were being checked at the door, separating the simply curious from the intended. From out of her small clutch, Dawn found the invitation given to her by Ava. At the door, it was carefully inspected, the doorman noting the specialness of this particular invite. With an extra bit of attention thrown our way, we were ushered inside. We each grabbed a flute of Riesling, nodding pleasantly at the other guests and trying our best to fit in.

"Um . . . I have a feeling the cost of these pieces tonight might be beyond our budget, Chase," Dawn said discreetly as she put the glass to her lips.

"You might be right," I said, reflecting on my employment limbo. "Want to get out of here?" I asked for other selfish reasons. A final try.

Dawn lowered her glass, looking at me stone-faced. "C'mon now. How would that look?" she asked.

"Hey. Just a suggestion," I offered with a grin and a shrug.

"I didn't squeeze into this dress for nothing, Chase. And it would be really rude to come all the way here and not take it all in."

"Okay. Where do you want to start?" I asked.

As Dawn scanned our surroundings, attempting to fathom where to begin on our journey of discovery, I observed the other guests and random art aficionados. It felt good that, despite her instability, Ava had really channeled her creativity and passion into something that was lauded and appreciated by so many. I nodded imperceptibly to myself, a strange sense of pride welling up as I drank deeply from my glass.

Mingling among the ever-moving throng of folk was a gentleman whose height set him apart. I clenched my teeth, knowing this would be the first of many challenges if we were to remain much longer. Smith Sampson had to be here as Ava's patron. I'm sure he was carefully orchestrating tonight's event, his pride certainly more appropriate than mine. Despite his being overdressed the first time we met, this time he stood out for being underdressed. The tall, thin ghostly pale man wore a white button-down shirt, a simple pair of blue jeans, and comfortable loafers. With his wire-rimmed glasses, he was almost more tenured professor than privileged eccentric. Not one for complete simplicity, he had a bright red scarf draped around his wrinkled, elongated neck.

He noticed me and smiled. Rather than running away, I gently guided the still-undecided Dawn in his direction. As he came closer, I saw he was going to speak. I decided to engage him first.

"How are you this evening, sir?" I asked, smiling cordially and speaking loud enough to bring Dawn's attention in his direction. I noticed her eyes taking in the strange visual that was Smith's.

"Things are going extremely well for Ms. Nuttier, so I have no complaints," he said with a giggle. I remembered the disdain he had for using her pseudonym when we met. "Smith Sampson," he said, offering his hand once again for the first time.

"Chase Hidalgo," I answered, shaking firmly. "And this is my wife, Dawn."

"Ahh. Dawn to the night. What a lovely vision you are, dear. Totally enchanting," Smith said as he clasped her extended hand in both of his. "I noticed you across the room and had to come over. That dress is adorable, absolutely adorable." Smith pivoted back toward me. "You are a lucky man to have such a woman, Mr. Hidalgo," he commented, using similar words as he'd reserved for Ava the day we first met.

"Thank you," I replied, our eyes meeting.

"Is this your gallery, Mr. Sampson?" Dawn asked.

"Heavens no," Smith scoffed. "My marriage of art appreciation and business acumen isn't so refined, I'm afraid. I'm simply here to support Ms. Nuttier on one of her biggest nights. And I'm glad the two of you were able to come out as well. Be sure to talk with her. She's terribly busy, but she'd love a moment with someone who's not a stuffed shirt."

"Why thank you. We'll be sure to do that," Dawn replied before I could think of what to say.

Smith gave the two of us a light pat on our backs and was off to interact with others. I was left unscathed, except for sweaty palms, which I discreetly rubbed on my pants legs.

Grabbing a refill of Riesling from a passing tray, we carried on with the viewing of Ava's works, a variety of images dispersed and hung about on the fourteen-foot-high walls of the gallery. Some I recognized from Ava's special room back at her place. They'd been stacked, probably in preparation for tonight's event. It was unseemly pretending they were all new to me, but I'd become comfortable with the lies and pretense.

We settled in front of the lighthouse painting, the one with the unusual-shaped boats drifting along below. I grinned, seeing the piece was still titled *Happiness.* Just like Ava wanted.

"Wow. She really takes you there. Wherever t*here* is," Dawn offered softly as she squinted, lost in the brush strokes. "You can tell she's seen a lot, even if it's all not easily understood."

"That's one way to put it," a woman's voice said just behind us. I flinched, heart surging as I turned to see to whom it belonged. I cursed internally that I recognized her. And she recognized me, perhaps feeling the same shock and disdain. How could employer and employee not know one another?

Maryann Milner, one of the senior partners at the firm—specifically, the one I was looking at when I crudely admitted beating Iris's husband down, was in attendance tonight with her partner of the domestic sort. Could this get any more awkward for either of us?

"Hey, Maryann," I said, beaming with false joy over one of the people who held my future in their hands. Remembering my mood when I stormed out of the office, she had to be taken aback by my demeanor. I gave her a hug anyway, now worried about an additional lie for Dawn to learn of. "I'd like you to meet my wife, Dawn."

"Hello," Maryann said to my wife, cordial enough. She then introduced us to her partner Sue, a stylish middle-aged Pakistani woman with an English accent.

"I didn't know you were into the arts, Chase," Maryann said, her eyes scanning the varied canvasses and probably looking to add to her collection.

"I'm full of many surprises. It just takes giving me a chance," I responded, a bit of unspoken pleading for my job creeping in.

"It's nice to meet someone from Chase's office besides Jacobi," Dawn joked as she leaned past, sending a shudder through me. "I keep telling him he should finish law school, then sit for the bar."

Okay. Dawn had enough drinks for the night. Now I was beginning to get pissed off.

Maryann cast a glance in my direction, perhaps looking for instruction on how to proceed. I kept my simple smile plastered across my face. "Well, perhaps when the time is right, Chase will listen to his better half," Maryann joked back, letting me off the hook. "It was nice meeting you, Dawn."

Moving on, we made our way past several more works of art with no further uncomfortable encounters.

"See anything you like?" I asked.

"A couple. But I want to see the rest on the other wall. Think we can negotiate for one?"

"You never know," I said slyly, refraining from revealing the inside track I had with the artist. *Once* had, I should say. If any amount could get us out of here with a damn painting and our marriage intact, I would pay it.

"Look!" Dawn blurted out, tilting her wine flute as if proposing a toast.

I quickly cast my gaze in the direction of her attention. I focused on the wall above the mingling bodies, not seeing anything of note. But Dawn wasn't looking at one of the art pieces. She was focused on a small crowd gathered in the corner . . . and on the ethereal form in the center of that crowd. A woman who was clad in black politely conversed and posed for pictures from amateur and professional alike. As if some secret frequency were broadcast that only she could hear, she broke from one of her soft smiles and slowly turned in our direction. It was as if she felt that crackle of electricity across the room. Like I had on a street corner late one night. A night that changed my life.

Her face revealed familiar longing as our eyes met.

"It's her. Charla Nuttier. C'mon!" Dawn blurted out as she yanked me toward the woman who had been my lover . . . and yet something more.

23

"She looks kinda busy," I told Dawn as we wove our way toward the artist Charla Nuttier. Suddenly my suit felt two sizes too small. I wanted to tighten my grip on Dawn's hand and flee this damned bright, happy gathering. It wasn't the brilliant artist, but rather the woman Ava that I feared tonight.

"I just want to say hi. Won't take but a second," Dawn replied, prodding me along. A couple was taking a camera-phone picture with Ava. A bundle of serious sexy, she stood between the two elderly aficionados, wearing a strapless black ruffled cocktail dress just for her occasion. Her ebony hair was pulled back in a ponytail with a stargazer lily tucked neatly just above her ear. She posed for the picture, but eyes were locked on me.

Unwavering.

Unrelenting.

Wanting.

But I'm a man and I needed to steel myself.

"She keeps looking this way," Dawn said, aware of it as well.

"Probably recognizes you from the supermarket," I offered.

We waited patiently for our turn with Ava. I kept my head low, visualizing being somewhere else. When the crowd broke, I let Dawn introduce me, playing the role of the dumb husband.

"Ms. Nuttier," Dawn began as she reached out for Ava's

exposed shoulder. A shoulder I knew just how to touch. Ava waved at somebody across the gallery, then gave her full, undivided attention to Dawn.

"Please," she chided. "Like I told you at HEB that day, call me Charla."

Dawn's face went flush with excitement over Ava remembering her. Had she been stalking my wife before I ended our relationship? My supply of nervousness and fear began to dissipate; anger and outrage filling my tanks instead. "Well, *Charla*," Dawn continued after instruction, "this is my husband Chase. I have to admit, I hadn't heard of you. He's the person responsible for introducing me to your work."

"Not really," I quickly offered as I shook Ava's hand, breaking away lest any chemistry or familiarity stand revealed. Tried to ignore the Lola by Marc Jacobs perfume I got a whiff of. "Just saw some stuff of yours at the Breakfast Klub and looked you up on the Internet. My wife is the art person."

"Oh, really? And what do you do, sir?" Ava said, playing the game as she stared at me quizzically.

"My job? I—"

"No," she said, waving a dismissive hand with a chuckle as she cut me off. This persona tonight was far more confident than the woman from which I pried myself away the other night. "I meant what is your *passion*, sir? What really gives your life purpose and fulfillment? What gets your blood going?"

A fertile pause hovered among us. Dawn's eyes squinted as she monitored this odd exchange. The hairs rose on the back of my neck as a plethora of images bombarded my memory. But I ignored them and the baser instincts that accompanied them. With the remainder of my Riesling, I tipped the glass toward Dawn.

"When you put it that way, I guess I'd say my wife is my passion," I answered with a smart smile.

Dawn gave me a kiss on the cheek while Ava glared from behind a mask of false approval.

"The two of you are too cute," Ava said. "Reminds me of the relationship my best friend Ava has with the man of her dreams. A match made in heaven stronger than any obstacles ever thrown at them. All of you are so lucky."

"Thanks," Dawn replied as I winced over Ava's testimonial about her *friend*. "Y'know, when my husband first saw your picture, he thought maybe you attended college with us at Sam Houston."

Ava grinned, looking dead at me. "No. I'm not from around here. Maybe your husband was thinking of someone who favors me."

"Maybe. I was just telling him how beautiful you are in person. I'm still amazed that we'd run into one another in a grocery store. Do you live in Spring?"

"No, no. I just happened to be in the area. And you struck me as such a nice person. Both you and your mother-in-law, Miss Earnestine."

She knew my mom's name. Why was she doing this to me?

"Well, again, I'm so thrilled that you invited us. Your work is incredible," Dawn responded, carrying on as if they were old friends. Could've imagined them growing into women together in the dorms back at Sam Houston. They were alike in several ways, besides their connection to a weak man, yet different.

"Thank you so much. I'm glad that you were able to make it. You have no idea how much good it does my heart to see you . . . and your husband here tonight. I have to meet the other guests, but we'll talk later about which painting you like best. Enjoy yourselves, you two. "

Dawn waited for Ava to move on, but was steady tapping her sandaled foot. After another moment of not a word being said, she turned to look at me. "If I didn't know better, I'd swear she was flirting with you."

"Yeah right," I said with a sneer as I took Dawn's wineglass away. "Let's finish looking at her artwork."

Ignoring me, Dawn continued. "Don't you think she's attractive?"

"She's attractive, I suppose. But go easy with the wild theories. I'm not her type," I answered, sparing much emotion.

"Oh? And what do you think is her type?"

Someone not trudging through life like me, I thought without saying. "Probably some mega-successful entrepreneur with six-pack abs."

"Well, you've got the abs, Chase."

"And with your motivation, I'm sure I'll get to the success part too," I added, more as a joke to lighten the mood . . . and deflect.

"Does that mean you're going to go back and finish law school?" Dawn asked, a discernible gasp escaping her mouth before I could say something. "Is *that* what that lady from your law firm was hinting at?"

I'd deflected, but not in the way I'd planned. "Can't say," I replied coyly as I heard those notes from when I played the piano at Ava's.

A sign.

But it wasn't me this time. Or a simple memory.

It really was playing.

It was the instrumental to Tupac's song playing as a selection for her show.

For me.

She knew I'd come.

Total manipulation.

I clenched my fist, realizing how stupid I'd been all along.

"Hey, honey. Why don't you get us some more Riesling?" I asked of my wife. "I need to talk to someone about a piece of art."

24

I quickly found her. She'd reunited with Smith Sampson near the gallery entrance. He was about to introduce her to another Houston power couple who'd recently arrived.

"I need to talk to you. Now," I stressed, grabbing Ava abruptly by her arm. Smith Sampson opened his mouth to object. I bared my teeth, looking for a fight even if it would be one-sided. I was good for that, as Iris's husband learned.

"It's all right," Ava said as she raised her hand to assuage her patron and friend. Smith quickly turned to the couple, presumably coming up with a diversion or excuse for Ava's sudden unavailability. With Ava stumbling, I pulled her along, determined to find an away spot.

"Chase—" she began to say.

"Shut up," I hissed gruffly. Just my luck, Maryann Milner was in the vicinity and witnessed the exchange. Her face looked more aghast than it did back in our office conference room that night. I could do nothing but groan and plod forward, knowing my days at Casey, Warner & Associates might be numbered.

But fuck it. And fuck doing things for other people.

Rounding a display wall, we almost ran into Dawn, who was looking for me, no doubt. She had two flutes of Riesling, our refill, and was drinking from one as she sauntered around. I stopped abruptly, reversing course in a nanosecond. Ava wasn't as quick to adjust and ran into me as I turned. I caught her long enough to steady her wavering form before charging off once again in a different direction.

"You're hurting my wrist, Chase," Ava said under her breath as I spotted the rear exit to the gallery. I eased up slightly on my grip so as to not alarm the guests as we pushed past them. This place wasn't big enough for me to avoid Dawn indefinitely, so this had to be short and sweet.

Well, maybe not so sweet.

I pushed the rear door open with my free hand, preparing for an alarm to sound as I shoved Ava ahead of me. It didn't come. The only thing greeting us was two startled staff members on cigarette break. I eyed them down as they recognized that they had somewhere else to be. Quickly extinguishing their smokes—one of which looked to be a joint—they returned inside to their duties.

Free of prying eyes, I dropped any pretense of being happy. Ava's attempt at a smile only threw gasoline on my fire.

"I've missed you," she said, nervously adjusting her dress for no reason. It still fit in all the right places.

"I told you it was over, Ava! Over! Then you pull this shit? You've been following my wife? And talking to my mom? *My family*? What were you trying to do tonight?"

"I'm sorry, Chase."

"No, you're not. Otherwise you wouldn't have invited Dawn here. You hurt me, Ava."

"That wasn't my intent. I just need your love," she said, moving to make the five feet between us less than five. "That's all."

"You need help. That's what you need."

"Then help me. Make me right, Chase."

"Stop. Stop," I said, waving my hands in front of her

to halt her advance. "When I leave here tonight, I don't want either me or my wife—or even my mom—ever hearing from you again. Got it?"

"What about your dad?"

"*Excuse you*?" I muttered, irate with Ava's myriad surprises and manipulations. "What do you know about my dad? I know you couldn't follow him too."

"Joell? Why wouldn't I know him? He's my father-in-law, dammit! The man you idolized. He taught you how to play the piano. That thing you're so afraid of for some reason."

"See. That's where you're wrong. I never idolized that man. Never. And he never taught me to play. I taught myself. And you know why? Because he wasn't around! My dad is a selfish fuckin' bastard. And he's not your father-in-law! I've been married only once in my life. And it's to that woman inside," I said, pointing toward the gallery as a pang of guilt set in the pit of my stomach. "You need to cut the bullshit! I don't know you and you never knew me!"

"That—that's not true. I do know you. I love you, Chase. And Joell is a good man. He's kind, a good husband, and a successful musician. He's all the things you are. And why I love you so much."

"Stop. Just stop. My dad lives virtually on the street these days. The last time he was a 'success' I was in elementary school. And even then he had no time for me or my mom. He disgusts me. Don't you ever talk to me about me being like him."

Ava trembled as she stared into my eyes. It felt as if the temperature dropped ten degrees. "Please don't leave me. You're all I have in this world," she said as her voice cracked.

"Then you have nothing," I said. Tears streamed down her face as I deflected her outstretched hand.

As before at her place, Ava tried to stop me from leaving again. This time she was more forceful as she shoved me repeatedly. Each time, I'd resume my stride toward the gallery while trying to refrain from reacting. To say her tears and pleas weren't twisting me up would be a lie. When I successfully got by her, she grabbed my jacket and yanked me back. I pulled free of her grasp, causing Ava to flop backwards on the gravel. She yelped in pain before quickly getting back to her feet. Tears were flowing more freely now. As she brushed off her legs, the beautiful stargazer lily dropped from her hair, landing between us. I almost stepped on it.

Something about seeing her beauty diminished, the utter despair on her face, sapped my will. But I wasn't some savior. I bent down to pick up her flower, considering urging her to seek help with her doctor.

But needing help myself.

Ava came close, fighting her tears and muffling her sniffles. She rested a hand on my shoulder while I was still down on one knee. I tried to focus on the lily, losing myself in its simple elegance for fear of being frozen by her gaze. She moved her hand from my shoulder and slid it up my neck, where it came to rest on the back of my head. She ran her hands through my hair, gently coaxing my head closer. Before I knew it, the side of my face was pressing against her crotch. I let the lily fall from my hand.

"Stop it, Ava," I requested, closing my eyes. She didn't relent, continuing to run her fingers through my scalp. Instinctively, I turned my head inward, breathing deeply through the fabric of her cocktail dress as I wedged my face between her legs. The Lola by Marc Jacobs perfume was there as well. Her warmth was more intoxicating; threatening to overwhelm me. I nudged the short dress, easing it up until my nose and lips were nuzzled against the outline of her mound. I probed against the black thong just as the headlights of a car being valet-parked briefly illuminated us.

"You got me wet as soon as I saw you tonight," Ava said, ignoring any fear of us being caught. "Taste me, Chase. Please. Taste me like you're dying of thirst and only I can quench you."

I clamped my lips together, catching her clit ever so briefly. A low purr escaped from deep within Ava as her legs trembled. More forceful kisses and sucking followed. I moved her thong aside. Doing this right here, right now, was already insane and foolhardy. Maybe just a taste would quench me. Maybe I'd have to have more. Already knowing the answer, I licked Ava, running my tongue up and down her pussy.

"Oooh. O—o—oh," she murmured as she draped one leg over my shoulder, wrapping it around my head as if a yoga master. I grabbed her ass cheeks to steady her as I continued to feast. "Please. Don't stop. Not tonight. Mmm. This is my night. *Our* night, baby."

Coming down off an orgasm, Ava pulled on my jacket again. Rather than trying to stop me from leaving now, she wanted me free, unrestrained.

I stood up, quickly removing my jacket. I set it on a nearby crate as Ava released my shirt from my pants and began unbuckling my belt. She pulled my pants and underwear down, exposing my hardened dick to the night air. She licked her lips seductively at the sight of me wanting her.

I grabbed Ava by her shoulders, forcing her back against the outer brick wall of the gallery. Our bodies slammed together abruptly as I brought my lips to hers. The kiss was rough and animalistic, lips being bitten and tongues plunging deeply. She moaned as I pushed up firmly against her. As our chests rose and fell, there wasn't an inch separating us. We were one as before.

"Put—put it in. Before we get caught," she urged, hearing the voices just inside the gallery's back door. Perhaps it was another worker wanting to go on smoke break. Maybe they were listening to us.

I pressed against Ava again, sliding my dick inside her inviting harbor. She was already so wet, wave after wave of her honey attempting to capsize my ship. But I held steady on my course, guided by instincts more sexual than nautical. She closed her eyes, throwing her head back as I pumped harder and harder. The eruptions came more often, more violently, as she caromed off the unyielding brick and mortar behind her. I held her aloft, her feet dangling and kicking as she sought to ride me to the ends of the Earth.

I was in a maddened state.

Going harder.

Deeper.

Trying to exact revenge for what she'd put me through as well as exorcise whatever unseen forces held me in her sway. She looked into my eyes, seeing something that pleased her with such delight that she cackled. Insanity was almost a certainty with her. But I was equally not of right mind.

"Do it. Do that shit," she cursed, throwing her head back again as she held onto my neck.

I felt my legs tighten as Ava bounced onto me, working to coax my seed from deep within my loins. She wrapped her legs around my waist, denying me any escape. I worked back against her, gripping her hips tightly as I matched her intensity. My balls slapped against her ass with every vigorous upstroke, robbing her of any voluntary response the more I pumped. She was my puppet, melting into me by way of our ravenous union. We both grunted as we tumbled headlong into the abyss.

"I—I."

"Uh-huh. Oh yes, Chase," she moaned, her words joining in the moment.

Then it was set free.

I stopped breathing in that moment of release. Eyes blinking. Frozen in time as I erupted inside her. Joining with the woman who swore we were already joined.

And just as sudden as it had begun, I regretted it.

Wanted to retract what had occurred as though it were a simple slip of the tongue.

Except it wasn't words that were damning or unfortunate.

It was actions.

I slowly eased off Ava, allowing her to regain her footing. Her breathing was still ragged, but she was more aware of her surroundings too. Her eyes darted about as she quickly lowered her cocktail dress, maybe a hint of embarrassment finally rearing its head. I pulled up my pants and hurriedly tucked my shirt back. I reeked of this woman, wiping away the sweat and lipstick from my face as if my obvious guilt could be just as easily removed. As Ava put her thong back on, I donned my jacket again and waited for her to finish making herself presentable.

"You ready?" I asked, once I assured her most of the brick dust had been wiped off her back and dress. Ava nodded, neither one of us comfortable talking at the moment. As paranoid as I'd been upon arriving at the gallery, now things were off the scale.

I opened the rear door for Ava, letting her rejoin her adoring guests first. Taking a moment to catch my breath, I followed several minutes later, preparing to rejoin a woman I didn't deserve and get the hell out of Dodge.

Once inside, I found Dawn easily. She held two now-empty wine flutes in her hands, eyeballing me as I emerged from the rear of the gallery. I had to look disheveled, despite a quick stop in the restroom to wash my face and regroup.

"Where have you been?" she asked, glaring at me.

"Trying to see if these prices are negotiable," I answered. "I had the hardest time finding someone who knew. Then I had to go to the restroom." I forced myself to end it there before my guilt set me to rambling.

"And?"

"And what?"

"What did you find?"

"Stuff is too high. You ready to go?" I asked, maintaining my distance.

"Yes. I think I've had enough wine."

"Me too," I said as I forced a smile to form on my face.

"Don't you want to say bye?"

"Uh . . . to who?"

"Charla?"

"No. You're her invited guest. But I'm sure she won't miss us."

Dawn's facial expression changed. Was hard to read. Maybe it was the alcohol. "Did you see all the paintings tonight?"

"No."

"There's one I found pretty interesting. Ran dead into it when I couldn't find you," Dawn offered. "C'mon, I'll show you on the way out."

I motioned for Dawn to lead, still afraid of her catching a whiff of Lola by Marc Jacobs on my clothes or *Charla Nuttier by Ava* on my body.

We made our way to the southeast corner of the gallery, not far from the exit through which I'd yanked Ava. Beneath a soft, recessed light was a painting I'd surely missed. Most of the crowd was gathered in other spots, so it left us virtually alone to take it in.

Piano in the Dark 141

"Now what is so special about this one—" I asked before abruptly ending my question midstream. I almost pissed on myself.

"You tell me," Dawn huffed as my mouth hung suspended in disbelief.

The sole object on the canvass was a man—a content figure wearing a contemplative smile.

A man who bore a striking resemblance to me.

"Look familiar?" Dawn asked, as if interrogating me. "That's you, isn't it?"

Before I could elicit some sort of feeble answer, we were disturbed by someone coming our way. It was Ava, Smith Sampson, and about four or five others. When Ava saw me and Dawn gathered in front of the painting, she stopped dead in her tracks, fumbling for words. The lily was missing from her hair, left outside in our haste. I don't think she expected to run into me so soon after. No one with half their sense could mistake the postcoital glow or the way she looked at me.

No one.

Not even the woman with whom I stood.

Oh, no.

When I turned back to Dawn, she'd dropped the wine flutes to the ground at my feet. Her breathing was so labored as to remind me of an enraged bull. She didn't have to explain the look in her eyes that differed wildly from Ava's. Betrayal was the sharpest of weapons, sometimes cutting the person that wielded it.

"You bastard!" Dawn yelled.

"No—wait—I—"

There was no forgiveness felt in the vicious slap my wife delivered across my face.

25

I blinked my tear-filled eyes, jaw smarting from what felt more like a fist than an open hand. "Baby, wait," I called out to Dawn as she left my side, fleeing the gallery and the embarrassment it had to represent. To think, she was so happy when this evening began. Now my irrational actions had finally taken their toll.

I took a final look back at the painting, knowing I never posed for it. Was it another part of Ava's trap for me tonight? Did she intend on Dawn seeing it? Did Dawn even know what had just occurred out back with Ava and me?

Didn't matter.

All was damaged, never to be put back together again.

Ava abandoned her circle of people and ran over, impeding my path to my wife.

"Chase—I—"

"Move!" I screamed, having zero appreciation at the moment for the conflicting emotions she elicited from me. The ring on my hand bound me to another, no matter what fantastic, arousing tales Ava could conjure. With that same hand, I shoved her aside. There was only one Mrs. Hidalgo and she'd just walked out on me.

"Now see here," Smith crowed as he came to his friend's aid with fists raised. I had no intention of physically harming Ava, but he couldn't know that. Especially with how I'd yanked her away earlier. I quickly backslapped him, sending him wobbling. His ridiculousl red scarf came unraveled. Gasps rang out in the gallery.

"You believe her shit? None of this is real, dude. None of it," I yelled at Smith while motioning at the works of Charla Nuttier all around us. I chuckled out of frustration, way past being simply *on edge.* "This stuff doesn't exist . . . never happened. What's real is my wife out there. Now get the fuck out of my way."

Smith complied, reaching for Ava, whom he embraced and began rubbing her back. A fleeting glance at the wounded Ava and I ran off in search of Dawn. The last thing I heard was someone asking if the police were needed.

My wife was standing near the valet stand, talking rapidly into a cell phone. When she saw me, she turned her back and said something to the valet. The tanned dude immediately looked in my direction, glaring at me. Now I had to go through this.

I took a circuitous route, wishing Dawn would acknowledge me. I raised my hands, palms out like some hostage negotiator approaching a loaded weapon.

"Chase, stay back," she said, trying to maintain some decorum in front of folk.

"C'mon. Let me take you home, baby," I said as I reached out. Mere inches from my touch, she retreated. The valet to whom she'd whispered a second ago uttered something to the rest of his crew in Spanish too rapid for me to *comprende.*

"You sure you don't want to go home with your mistress?" she taunted, handing back the phone to the valet attendant.

"Dawn, you don't know what you're talking about."

"Don't I?" she responded. "First, she flirts with you in my face. Then I see how she was just looking at you. My momma didn't raise a fool. When did you pose for the painting, Chase? Huh? One of those nights you were working late on a big case?"

"That—that's not me in that painting. All of this is blown out of proportion."

Dawn chuckled. "You're an awful liar. Jacobi didn't teach you how to all these years? I mean . . . you're his flunky, his protégé . . . his stooge. How long have I been a fool?"

I bowed my head, contrition before confrontation. "Dawn . . . please," I begged.

"Go to hell!" she lashed out.

I reacted to a shrill whistle that came from the driveway. A yellow minivan taxicab had arrived. The head attendant, without leaving Dawn's side at his post, waved his hand for it to pull up.

"Sir, I need you to clear the driveway," he instructed as I heard the taxi's engine rev. I remained in place, fearing I might never see my wife again if I let her leave like this. Three more valet attendants joined their supervisor, forming a loose wall between me and her. With the taxi unable to proceed without running me over, they pivoted to allow Dawn to walk by and go to the car, while keeping me at bay.

"Dawn, c'mon! Let's go somewhere and talk," I threw out. When the sliding door was opened for her, I tried lunging past her human wall, but was shoved back. A brawl certainly wouldn't help my case.

"Sir, please step back," one of them said.

"Fuck you!" I spit. As Dawn was driven off, I produced my claim ticket from my wallet, flinging it at them. "Get me my fuckin' car, now!"

"You need to calm down first. Have you been drinking?"

"What are you? My fuckin' AA sponsor? There's my ticket. Now get me my damn car." I could see the cab put on its signal to turn onto Taft. If I hurried I might be able to follow. I removed my jacket in frustration while the lead attendant fetched my keys and handed them off to another.

As the man left quickly around back, two sets of bright headlights descended on me. As I focused beyond them, I could make out familiar red and blue lights on the rooftops twirling round and round. I looked at the lead attendant, rolling my eyes. Now he chose to smile. Asshole.

The dual Houston Police Department cruisers formed in a pincer move on me, both quickly coming to a stop. I put my hands in front of my face to shield my eyes. More patrons from inside the gallery had exited to witness the commotion. At this moment, I cared not if Ava were one of them.

"Sir, is there a problem?" one of the two officers asked. He was short and built like a fireplug. A neck was a luxury not afforded him.

"No, officer. There is no problem. I just need my car so I can leave."

His shoulder-clipped radio chirped, to which he clicked on it and spoke in code. "We got a disturbance call with a possible assault. Would you happen to know anything about that?"

"No," I succinctly replied. The lead valet attendant walked over, speaking in whispered tones with the officer closest to me. The officer responded by giving a nod to his partner.

"Sir, I'm going to need to see some ID as well have you get down on the ground. We just need to clear this up. Can you do that for me?"

"I'm not getting on the ground like some criminal because I haven't done anything, officer. That little guy has my keys around back and I just need my car so I can go. No problems."

The two moved in sync so fast that I was startled. By

my last syllable, guns were already drawn and fixed on me. Yep. It was going down.

And not in a good way.

"Sir, get down on the ground!"

"Aww, c'mon now—" I yelled just as triggers were pulled.

They fired away, sending high voltage through the little wires that had sought me out.

I involuntarily met the ground, losing total control of my body in the process.

I'd never been tazed before.

For the record, the shit totally sucked.

26

After an uncomfortable overnight stay in the Harris County jail, the judge informed me and my attorney at my side that I was free to go. The police found no weapons on me and no one from the gallery had come forward to press charges. *Fascinating* was the only word my weary mind could summon. Not what I would use to describe my current situation, but it was the sole word my troubled cell mate repeated all night—fascinating, fascinating, fascinating.

"Fuckin' cops tazed me. What about that?" I mumbled.

"Shhh. Just be quiet and look appreciative," Jacobi whispered through his teeth as we listened to the judge's stern warning about my behavior and his sincere hope that he never see me in this setting again. He had reason for saying that. Judge Thomas Rowe was at TSU Law School the same time as the two of us. Another example of my failings, as Dawn would remind me.

Dawn.

While assholes argued, fought or simply kept repeating words last night, I thought of my wife. Kept seeing that damn yellow cab as it pulled off. Remembered the smell and texture of us walking into our new home for the first time. Had flashes of us feeding one another wedding cake at the reception hall in Humble. Thought of our magical wedding before it and those eternal two words: I do.

I didn't hear a thing Jacobi said on the elevator ride down at the Harris County Criminal Courts. At least my boy's black eye had healed. And they allowed him to return to work in spite of the Iris debacle. Things looking up for somebody, I suppose. I wondered what kind of story he'd cooked up to appease them.

"Hey. You listening?" my friend asked as we descended toward the lobby.

"Huh?" I replied.

"Knew it," Jacobi said, allowing a chuckle to escape. "We need to get you cleaned up, man."

"I just want to go home, shower, and get some sleep."

"Not a good idea, bro. You know how it is with this domestic stuff. Let her cool off. Otherwise you might find yourself on Judge Rowe's bad side next time."

"Shit. Tommy's never had a good side," I responded.

Jacobi just shook his head and laughed, his eye on the floor numbers.

As we exited the elevator, someone called out to me. "Chase!" they uttered again. It was coming from the incoming line by the metal detectors and X-ray machines.

I closed my eyes for a second and centered myself, pretending it was Dawn, eager to take me back and try to work through this. I smiled, imagining my sheets, realizing how my bed would feel . . . especially with her beside me. But the hairs on the back of my neck spoke more loudly than my attempts at drowning out the actual voice.

"Ain't that your stalker, man?" Jacobi asked, compelling me to open my eyes.

It was Ava.

This woman. My lover rather than my wife, concerned for my welfare. Devotion devoid of the reality set before her.

Wow. Trip.

Absent any makeup or her Charla-Nuttier-big-time-artist-veneer of last night, she was still just as stunning. Seductive simplicity mixed with sadness that was hard to look away from.

And still fucked up my head.

Made me want to do things I good 'n well knew weren't right despite feeling otherwise. But for even the slightest chance of fixing things with Dawn, I had to be rational.

For once.

"Keep walking, bro," I said to Jacobi. "Just keep walking."

We exited out the front where gloomy, overcast skies never looked so good. Free of the courthouse, I turned on my phone once more in hopes Dawn had reached out. As we took the steps to the street below, I saw Ava briskly walking out the front door in pursuit.

"Hey. Give me a minute," I requested of Jacobi. He took one look at me, then glanced at the approaching Ava. "Won't take long," I reassured him.

"Seems you're having a hard time with decisions, bro," he offered. "Unless your mind is already made up and you haven't come around to admitting it." With that, he threw up his arms and continued his trek down the steps to wait on me.

I slowed for Ava to overtake me.

"Glad you're all right," she offered, giving me an awkward hug that I didn't return.

"Hope I didn't ruin your show."

"I apologized to everyone for the misunderstanding. Said it was my fault. But I'd trade a thousand gallery shows for you, Chase. I hope you know that."

"Why me?"

"Because it's always been you. And always will be."

"Again with the stuff that doesn't make sense. Just like that damn painting that got me in trouble," I sighed.

"This is costing you a bunch of pain, Ava. And it's not making my life much better. When I said to leave me and my family alone last night, I meant it."

"You mean before we made love? You and I both know that was incredible last night."

"That was lust . . . and misguided feelings."

"You know that's not true."

"Look. I'm just a man who wants to get his wife back, then work on turning the rest of his life around."

"And I just want what I once had."

"Well, I wish you the best with that, but I won't be a surrogate for your deceased husband. We don't always get what we want."

I began descending the steps, figuring there was nothing else to say. Nothing I could say.

"Chase, I might not be around here much longer," she blurted out. "I don't have as much time as I'd like. So forgive me for being so pushy."

I stopped on the landing below and eyed her again. *Manic desperation on her part?* I wondered to myself. "If you're talking suicide or something, don't do it. Life is too precious . . . no matter the circumstances. Get some help."

In an odd display, she smiled. Softly. Serenely.

"That's the Chase I know," she uttered from the top of the steps before walking off and disappearing from my sight. Blaming it on the morning haze and my exhaustion, I almost could've sworn she'd faded away momentarily, as if a mirage.

Rubbing my eyes, I scurried the rest of the way down the stairs to catch Jacobi.

27

"Whoa!" Jacobi exclaimed as he drove me to retrieve my car from the gallery. I'd explained what had been happening, including what led me to being tazed and locked up.

"And that's what you've missed," I said.

"So you fucked this girl at the gallery? While Dawn was there? And now this chick Ava shows up at the court-house to bail you out? After you sidelined her in front of everyone at the gallery to go chase your wife?" he rattled off laughingly. He went silent, digesting it for a second as we passed a group of bicyclists. "Dang. You a beast, son. Didn't think you had it in you."

"I don't, man. This ain't me. And you know that. I'm strong when I'm away from Ava. But when we're around one another, I get irrational and spontaneous. It's like something goes haywire inside me. Oh. Forgot to tell you. Maryann was there at the gallery last night."

"Milner?" Jacobi asked, turning his music down in the Range Rover for the first time. "From the office?"

"Bingo," I replied.

"Damn. Did she see any of this?"

"Probably. If I thought my job situation was tenu-ous before last night, now I'm really worried. You gotta help me, bro. Have you heard anything at the job?"

"No, nothing yet," Jacobi replied, oddly hesitating. He turned the music back up—B.o.B.'s "Nothin' on You" replacing Trey Songz's boasting of *the neighbors knowing his name while inventing sex and making you say ahh from yo side of the bed* or something. As we continued down Allen Parkway, Jacobi passed the Federal Reserve Building and slowed at Taft, but realized he'd have to go a little further before making a U-turn to get to the other side of the street.

"I need to come back, man. And not just for the paycheck. I need some stability and sanity right about now. If Dawn knew I've been on leave, she'd really be through with me."

"So it's not the infidelity, it's the finances? Your wife is harsh," he joked.

"A lie is a lie is a lie, man."

"Where you staying in the meantime?"

"Haven't given it much thought. Figured I'd try to go by the house and talk things over."

"And if not?"

"With me in job limbo, I can't afford to blow money on hotels. I already wasted some on the new car."

"Especially if Dawn's going to be splitting the property," Jacobi added in bad taste. "My crib is your crib, dude. Just don't touch my toothbrush . . . or my porn. No. Wait. I'll share my porn. You might need it more than me."

"Gee. Thanks," I offered, shaking my head as the reality that I might never be with Dawn again set in.

We made our way back down Allen Parkway, downtown bound, passing KHOU television studios before turning right onto Taft. Passing Gravitas where I'd shared my *last supper* with Dawn, Jacobi wheeled the Range Rover around to Rhode Place per my instructions.

"Is this where your car is supposed to be, man?" Ja-

cobi asked as he slowed outside the gallery. With it being closed, my car should've been easy to spot.

Except it wasn't there.

"Fuck me," I cursed.

28

After a hard day's work, the Spring Trails sign to my neighborhood off Riley Fuzzel Road usually brought me a sense of peace and relief. But today it was a source of great stress when Jacobi turned into the subdivision. Several calls to the tow companies had yielded no results and I refused to believe someone had stolen my new Acura TSX. That would be a serious case of *when it rains it pours*. And I was already in the monsoon with no raincoat.

So that left another alternative.

Go home and hope it was there.

And face my wife, hoping my marriage was there.

I nervously checked my phone for the third time in the last minute to see if Dawn had perhaps returned my call and I'd missed it. But no such luck was in store. After turning off Spring Trails Bend, we wound our way to my home on Julia Park Drive, where I spotted my car parked in the street. Rather than placing it in the garage or at least parking it in our driveway, Dawn left it discarded like some temporary nuisance.

"Mystery solved, my man. At least she didn't key it or bust out the windows," Jacobi offered as he slowly pulled into the driveway . . . our driveway.

I said nothing, instead looking at my car then back at the house before repeating the sequence.

"Need me to stay for a minute? Until you're on your way?"

I opened the door, cradling my car keys in my hand. "Nah. I got this," I replied. "I'll see you at your place in a little bit."

I stood in my driveway, staring at my home as Jacobi put the Rover in reverse. It would be so good to stand under the spray of my own shower right now and wash this jail funk off me. I checked my phone one more time. Nothing from Dawn. Resigning myself to the fact that the next call would be from some overpriced Post Oak Boulevard divorce attorney, I clicked the remote to my car.

"They were going to tow it," Dawn softly spoke from the porch, scaring the hell out of me. She still wore her dress from last night, albeit wrinkled. Her makeup remained only in streaks. A lit cigarette dangled between her fingers. My wife didn't smoke. "You should be thanking me for bringing it here . . . considering."

"Thank you," I said cautiously. No knife was visible in her other hand despite prior random warnings regarding infidelity . . . and what would happen to my testicles—snip, snip. Having seen Dawn also, Jacobi stopped backing up and lowered his window, awaiting further instructions. "Can we go inside and talk? Please, baby?" I begged.

"Why? There's nothing in there for you, Chase. Not anymore," she coldly stated. I took the greater meaning in her words, digesting the poison.

"I want to explain."

"So you can lie like that dog?" Dawn scoffed, her reddened eyes cutting at the Range Rover parked behind me.

"Hey, I got nothing to do with this, Dawn. Believe that," Jacobi called out, overhearing her.

"Fuck you!" she spat, flicking her cigarette in his general direction. He hurriedly raised his window back up.

I gave him a look to keep his window up and mouth shut. "Was your bitch following me in the store to rub it in my face? Was I some kind of joke to the two of you?"

"Look. I don't know about that painting, but I—"

"Don't play with me. I gives a fuck about that painting, Chase. I saw the look on her face at the gallery. I can't get it out my mind. I just can't. A woman knows when another woman wants what she has. Just be a man and tell me. Are you fucking her?"

"No—not anymore. It—doesn't make sense. Look. I don't know how this happened," I mumbled and stumbled. Before I could build a case, I'd already lost in the court of my wife's heart.

Unanimously.

All that was left was sentencing.

"You disgust me," she said from behind eyes holding a storm at bay. "I put together a bag of your shit. It's by the front door. Take it and get the fuck out of my face."

"No. Wait. I love you, Dawn. I'm not just going to give up on us," I said, recklessly trying to embrace her.

Stupid.

Dawn swung on me with a series of windmills, a primal growl escaping her throat that I'd never heard before. I had to put my arms up to shield myself. When I retreated a sufficient distance, she halted. Whatever rage she'd conquered since last night had erupted to the surface again.

"Look," she said, stabbing a finger at me as her makeup began to run again. "I told myself I wasn't causing a scene in front of the neighbors. And look what you had me do. You're not worth it. You don't deserve this, you cheating bastard! Now get your bag before I call the cops and you go to jail again. And believe me . . . Montgomery County won't be as nice to your black ass as Harris."

"Listen to her, bro," Jacobi feebly offered, having cracked his window just a smidge this time.

Accepting the moment, I walked to the front door where a hastily packed duffel bag lay on the hardwood floor. I glanced back at Dawn.

"The locks will be changed by this afternoon," she said.

29

"Hey, boy," she called out as I walked down the hallway toward her after exiting the elevator. She was suspicious. I knew that from the second her eyebrow twitched. Of course, the hand on her hip was another sign.

One of her coworkers sauntered by, same navy and powder blue uniform as my mom, but possibly Honduran by her features. In her gloved hand, she carried some sort of cleaning solution in an anonymous spray bottle. Just another day at an anonymous office building on the north loop for an anonymous cleaning crew. But my mom preferred to be unseen; the stark opposite of my dad who lived to bask in the adulation and praise of others.

Once.

"Hey, Mom," I responded. I gave her a swift kiss on the cheek in the hopes she'd loosen up. Would make it easier to talk to her. Maybe blunt her disappointment that was to come. But that was foolish of me. For my mom was no fool.

"Shouldn't you be at work?" she asked as she quickly rolled up the vacuum cleaner cord she'd unplugged from the wall outlet. I almost reached to help her, but she'd just slap my hand away.

"I'm off temporarily. Waiting to go back," I replied, cognizant of the old warm-ups packed for me by Dawn that I wore. Eventually I would need to gather some more clothes from home if Dawn hadn't burned them or donated them to Goodwill.

"I know they don't do layoffs over there. What did you do, boy?"

"Where do I start?" I offered glumly.

"Dawn called me crying," she admitted with a shake of her head and a tsk in her voice. "I take my break in about thirty minutes. Let me finish this floor. I'll meet you down in the lobby," Earnestine said.

We sat together on one of the brick-framed benches within view of the glass elevators transporting people to various floors. Sunlight filtered in from the skylights above. Earnestine had intently listened without commenting as I vomited out a majority of the details. When I was done, she checked her bun to make sure her gray hair was still secure. Then she turned and looked me square in the eye.

"Yep. That man's blood in you," she offered in such a matter-of-fact way that hurt worse than raising her voice ever could. I came here like a scared little boy seeking his mommy and had been lumped in undesirably with Joell by the one person whose approval I craved.

"I gotta make this right."

"She told me she kicked you out. Where you stayin'?"

"At my friend Jacobi's for now."

"Uh-huh," my mom threw out. "Your wife thinks he's to blame."

"He had nothing to do it. I promise. This was all my being stupid."

"You think you love her?"

"Dawn? Of course. Never stopped," I replied, brimming with conviction.

"No. I ain't askin' 'bout your wife. That art lady. She pretty. Pretty and strange. When we saw her in HEB, she was all close-up on me like we was kin or something. Way too comfortable. *Hmph.* Maybe she thought I was gonna be her future mother-in-law."

"In her mind, you already are," I mumbled, Ava's pervasive whispers in my head resurfacing.

"What did you say?"

"Nothing. Just crazy talk, s'all," I replied. "I got caught up, Mom. Now I have to fix things with Dawn. But it was like me and this woman just fit."

"I'll bet you did. Probably too much *fittin'*," she joked straight-faced. "Thought I raised you better."

I lowered my head, embarrassed. "You did, ma'am."

"You never answered me, though. Do you think you love this Ava woman? Something you need to know before you can fix stuff."

"I love Dawn," I quickly answered.

"It's like I'm looking at Joell all those years ago when you make that face. You still didn't answer my question, boy. Do you think you love—"

"It's over," I stressed, cutting her off. Very rude of me. "I promise."

"Okay. So you say it's over, boy," my mom stated as she stood up to return to work. "Now how you gonna handle this mess you created?"

30

"Uh-huh. Yes. Two-dozen roses," I requested into the phone on my lap. "Yes. Same as before—mixed yellow and red. To her work address and home address." I checked my watch again as the florist confirmed my order.

Same flowers. Every day.

And I would continue until Dawn agreed to speak to me.

From my car, I cast my gaze over the North Oaks Shopping Center parking lot at Veterans Memorial and FM 1960, waiting for him. This was one of his few predictable routines. I told myself I did this for my mom, but I cared for him too on some level, despite his failings. Even if he didn't know I was watching, I could assess his state and at least know he was still alive. But after the last hour, he hadn't shown up.

I went to start the car, dreading where I was about to go next. But my phone rang.

A call from work.

"About damn time," I muttered, feeling one of my many weights lessening. The job limbo was about to end. I cleared my throat, preparing to sound more professional than my scraggly demeanor today. My five o'clock shadow was more akin to nine o'clock eclipse and I needed a haircut badly. I turned it off speakerphone, raising it to my mouth to engage in a more personal conversation.

"Hello," I said after the third ring.

"What up, dude," Jacobi said in a low, measured tone. Could tell he was in his office, not wanting anyone to eavesdrop.

"Nothin'," I answered with a grimace. "I thought you were one of the partners."

"Not a partner yet," he glibly remarked. "Sorry."

"You got word for me? Did they tell you anything?" I asked desperately.

"Not yet. But I need your help with something."

"What?" I'd heard this way too often from my friend, but I bit my tongue. I needed my job. For me and Dawn.

"Sally is awful," Jacobi replied, referring to another one of the firm's paralegals. "They've got her covering for you. All my stuff is disorganized now. Is the Crosby case going to mediation?"

"No," I replied with a roll of my eyes he couldn't see through the phone. "The defense declined our sugges-tion. We're just waiting on a trial date."

"Okay, okay," he mumbled while probably jotting down a note on his calendar. "Um . . . is the dictation fin-ished on my case summary for Randazzo?"

"You never dictated a summary on that case, man."

"Oh," he chirped. Part of my job covering for Jacobi was dictating letters and such that he either forgot to do or was so awful at that I would edit.

Seeing my opportunity, I chose to turn the conver-sation back to something advantageous to me. "I can't help you as much from the outside. I need to be back at my desk, so we don't miss a beat. And it's been more than two weeks. Things are going to just get more dis-organized. The partners can't just leave me twisting in the wind like this. You gotta talk to them, man."

"I'm working on that, bro, but have some patience. Trust me. I ain't been back long myself. The thin ice is shared, believe that."

"Anything else you need? I'm kinda in the middle of something."

"What? More flowers for Dawn?" he clowned.

"Fuck you. I did that earlier."

"Okay," my temporary roommate said with a laugh. "You wanna eat out tonight? My treat, dawg."

"Not tonight. I don't know what time I'll be back," I answered, letting my frustration show in my voice. Since moving in with him, most of our dinners consisted of me being peppered with work questions by Jacobi to where I was doing his job . . . again. For some reason, stuff like that never bothered me in the past. But that was before Ava upended my life and made me reassess a lot. Could almost swear he was preparing himself for my permanent absence from the firm.

Ending my conversation with Jacobi, I left my vantage point, rolling past CiCi's Pizza. Across the parking lot, the discarded shopping cart by Smoothie King where my dad usually performed was still vacant. Leaving the shopping center, I turned right onto Veterans, venturing slowly south as I looked on both sides of the street for a familiar silhouette.

On the right side of the street, just past the comical restaurant shape that is Pirates Seafood Boat, the familiar faded golden glint brought a smile to my face and an equal sense of relief. I was worried for nothing.

But as I got a closer, I discerned the hand holding it wasn't my dad's.

A small group of boys, maybe in their teens, were laughing and joking among themselves as they ambled down the sidewalk toward me. One was counting some dollar bills, while another absentmindedly dangled a dented, weathered trumpet from his fingers. When it fell on the sidewalk, he stumbled over to pick it up, accidentally kicking it further along up the street.

No respect for it or the history it held.

Panic and rage inhabiting me, I firmly gripped the steering wheel as I pointed the car directly at the cluster and gunned the motor.

31

"Hey! What the fuck, man!" one of the crew yelped as I ran up on the curb, cutting them off. With the car still running, I jumped out to confront the puzzled teens.

"Where'd you get the trumpet, son?" I asked its temporary owner. He'd just snatched it back up off the pavement as I ran up on them.

"Dude back there gave it to me," he replied nonchalantly, not too concerned by my posture. Kid was accustomed to confrontation.

My dad would never part with that trumpet. At least, not willingly. In some bizarre way, it meant more to him than his family. I began to wonder if maybe that money one of them was counting might be my dad's too. I started looking for signs of a scuffle on their knuckles or clothes.

"You a cop?" the smallest one asked. Couldn't be more than fifteen.

"No," I answered, not taking my eyes off the trumpet.

"Then move the fuck out the way, man," he said with a sneer. The rest of them laughed and nodded.

I sized them up, debating my next course of action. Five to one, not counting possible weapons on them, but some of them would flee if something jumped off. The last few days had been too violent already.

"Tell you what. Give me the trumpet and I'll give you a twenty without anybody getting hurt. Deal?"

In seconds that felt like an eternity, I tensed as I removed the money from my wallet. In one hand, I held it out before the kid.

"Make it forty," he countered.

"Fuck you. And you better hope he's okay."

"Whatever, man," he said, snatching the money from my hand while dropping the trumpet again. When I bent down to retrieve it, they quickly ran off, jetting across the traffic on Veterans to disappear from my sight.

With a sense of urgency now, I jumped back in my car and quickly backed off the curb. I made the two blocks down Veterans to where I came upon Champions Business Park, a mixture of odd businesses and storage facilities. From memory, I sped down one of the streets between the structures, narrowly avoiding a car backing out of a transmission shop housed here.

When I got to the rear, I pulled over and parked. Somewhere along the fence was a cut portion leading to the adjacent apartment complex on Bammel North Houston Road. Probably where those kids who had his trumpet lived. Near this, my dad usually found a tiny space between the buildings to lay his head. In days when it was too cold, some of the shop owners were nice enough to let him sleep inside in exchange for watching their place after hours. The man still had fans, especially in the Hispanic community around here.

"Dad!" I called out, pacing carefully along the fence line while looking and hoping.

Nothing.

"Joell!" I tried this time. His trumpet was in my hand, an orphan eager to be reunited. I came closer to the fence, peering toward the apartments for any sign of movement or a cardboard box in which he might be holed up.

When I didn't see or hear anything, the thought of calling the police began to factor into my thinking. Before I went that far, I came up with a far-fetched idea. Grimacing, I took the trumpet and thoroughly wiped the mouthpiece. Who knew what dwelled on it or the last time it had been cleaned? Nevertheless, I put it to my lips, fingering the keys as I blew.

A few random notes from "The Girl from Ipanema" were all I could produce; an awful rendition of what he warmed up with.

But it served its purpose.

Gravelly laughter amid some coughing came from behind an old oil drum in a tiny alley between some storage buildings. I gladly removed the horn from my lips and ran toward the sounds.

Lying on his back with a lump over his eye was an alive Joell Hidalgo.

"Why you messin' up my song?" he groaned as I helped him to his feet. "Sound like shit."

"I was just returning this to you," I said with a smile. I quickly fixed my face back to the sternness to which he was accustomed.

"My baby always comes back," he uttered as he took the beat-up trumpet, cradling it in his scratched and scuffed arms as if the one true love of his life. I could see now that he had a busted lip. It would need to heal before he could entertain again at the shopping center.

"Uh . . . it almost didn't this time. You need to be more careful around here. You could've been killed."

"By who? Those punk kids?" he scoffed, rubbing his sore ribs. "I've been in worse fights in my sleep. How's your momma?" Earnestine ever on his mind.

"She's good. Look . . . I should get you to Houston Northwest," I said, referring to the nearest hospital. "There might be something broken or worse."

"Nah. What I need is a good shower. Ain't had one in—"

"Okay. Gotcha," I said, trying not to think about the smell. I usually kept my distance.

"You know I never want to bother you and that wife of yours."

"I know, Dad."

"But if you could spare a moment for me just to get cleaned up . . . maybe take a little nap . . ."

"*At my house?*"

Joell slipped into embarrassment. "Don't worry about it," he hastily whispered.

"No, no. That's not what I—"

"I said don't worry about it!" he growled, the erratic man who refused help returning.

"I'm not welcome at my house right now. The locks have been changed."

Joell stared at me, fighting to emerge from the haze that gripped his mind these days. "Y'all two . . .?" he asked apologetically. Could've easily been *y'all too*.

"We'll work through it, Dad."

"I'm sorry." Our eyes met through his phrase of regret, a connection made for the first time. "It's okay. I'ma make a call. See if we can get you that shower," I said as I led him to my car.

I made the call, as difficult as it was, and took my dad on a short drive. A brief respite from his existence. Anywhere too far from what he called his home and he became extremely unmanageable. A pity he never stayed on his meds.

At the house, I knocked on the door, having let its resident know we were there already.

As the front door opened, I tensed.

"Hey, boy," Earnestine said, embracing me. Looking at the smelly, troubled man behind me, she craned her neck. "Hello, Joell," she offered to her former husband in as cordial a manner as possible.

32

The next week, I sailed down Highway 59, heading to my office downtown, aloft from winds of good fortune for a change. I was subjecting myself to more traffic by taking the freeway from Jacobi's place, but wanted to avoid any trip through Midtown where complications in the form of a beautiful, perplexing woman dwelled.

"What do you mean you invited him over for dinner?" I asked my mother, who'd just hit me with a startling tidbit she chose to share.

"Boy, don't raise your voice with me."

"Sorry, Mom, but you know Joell can be dangerous," I offered, referring to his irrational outbursts in recent years. I was usually the one who had to squelch things with the police.

"Not with me."

"Not physically at least," I responded defiantly as the downtown Houston cityscape came closer into view.

"Chase, you saw how he was nothing but skin and bones when you brought him over that night. And with them boys stealing his tip money too? A damn shame. I wanted to cry."

"That's why I gave him what cash I had when I brought him back, Mom. Wasn't going to tell you, but I put him up for a night at the In Town Suites on 1960 too. He was too tired to refuse this once."

"And you shouldn't be spending your money, boy. Especially with that new car and your not working."

"That might not matter soon. My job called me in this morning. Matter of fact, I'm on my way there now."

"Praise, Jesus!" Earnestine exclaimed. "Did you tell Dawn?"

"Not yet. Things still rough between us. You talk to her?"

"Yeah. She strong. Copin'. Ain't saying much about you still."

"Hey, Mom."

"Yeah?"

"How could you ask Dad over?" I asked, still unnerved by it. "He doesn't own a phone."

"I asked him yesterday. You told me where he plays that damn horn. I caught him over by the Smoothie King sitting on a shopping cart. Just like you said. Lookin' like a fool trying to blow with that split lip. He sure ain't gettin' any tips that way. I don't know what made me go over there, boy," she replied in a whimsical tone. Sounded like a guilty schoolgirl. "Anyway, I felt sorry for him, Chase. He needs more than just money or shelter."

"He needs someone that cares for him," I said, completing the thought she wouldn't dare speak aloud.

"Now there you go startin' mess. I didn't say all that, boy."

"You didn't have to."

"Hush your mouth."

"Look. I can't tell you what to do—"

"Damn straight."

"But—"

"I know," she responded, ending our nonverbal conversation. "I love you too, my son. Now go focus on that job and make me proud."

Don't fuck this up. Don't fuck this up, I thought, taking several deep, cleansing breaths. I even splurged on a new suit for this meeting, my welcome back to Casey, Warner & Associates. In spite of my going through the motions for so long, I would rededicate myself to this job. Fuck Ava's ideas about what I should be doing. This was for me. I was going to claim it.

I was back in the conference room for another face-down, except the group of partners was missing some members for this go-round. Okay. Almost none of them—Jim Warner, Abner Casey, Maryann Milner—were present. That left a lone Rick Stein sitting across from me to discuss my future. The jacket to his pinstripe suit rested on the seatback. The sleeves on his crisp white shirt were rolled up, like he'd been toiling over this all morning.

Only one person needed for a firing. And best to let the most likable do it.

Fuck.

"Are you letting me go?" I asked bluntly. I think I wanted to faint.

"Relax, Chase," Rick said with a brief smile forming on his chubby face. "Jacobi went to bat for you and explained everything to us. While not happy with this at all, we're accepting you back. But on a probationary basis. As a favor to Jacobi and for recognition of the excellent work you've done over the years."

"Whew. Glad Jacobi explained my thought process during that incident. It's still no excuse."

"So you admit everything?"

"Yes. Sure . . . I guess. I lost my cool and overreacted. Just like I told you last time," I replied, referring to the beatdown of Iris's husband once again. Hopefully, this would be my final time revisiting it. "But perhaps I could've been more tactful and contrite before you guys. It reflected poorly on this firm. And I'll bust my ass to regain the firm's trust."

"We are all so glad to hear that, Chase. You can start by signing here," Rick said, sliding the drafted agreement forward along with a pen. "And although we understand your need to be contrite, your sleeping with that woman was—"

"Huh?" I said, holding the pen suspended above the agreement.

"Your extramarital affair, Chase. I was referring to that part in all this."

"*In all this?* Wait. How much did Jacobi tell you?" I asked, irate that my friend had shared so much of my private affairs with these people. Or maybe it was Maryann who saw more of me and Ava at the gallery than I suspected. Would explain why she wouldn't want to attend this meeting. I was sloppy and careless that night.

"Everything. He told us everything, Chase."

"Wow," I said with a low gasp. "But I'm not quite sure how any of that has to do with my job."

"Barring your other dalliances, it does when one involves this firm's client and one of our lawyers is assaulted while trying to end things discretely on your behalf."

"Client? Who was assaulted? I'm totally confused now."

"Iris Garcia-Wilson. The woman whose husband you beat up. The woman whose relationship with you Jacobi attempted to cover up. He was reluctant to reveal the details, but finally enlightened us upon his return. Until that moment, we thought he was the guilty party and, as one of our lawyers, were prepared to deal with him accordingly. You have a true friend to take a black eye for you and keep their mouth shut about it for so long."

"My relationship with Iris . . ." I repeated in a daze as I saw my friend's smile and his telling me to trust him. I stabbed the pen into the paper, refusing to move it.

"Is something wrong, Chase? Is something incorrect in the agreement we drafted?"

"No . . . no. I just—I need to speak with Jacobi for a minute before I sign this."

"This is highly unusual, but you know where his office is."

"I most certainly do," I responded, standing up and removing myself from the conference room.

A room to which I knew I wouldn't return.

33

Our receptionist Kelli Jo was waiting for me in the hallway when I emerged from the conference room with the unsigned agreement in hand. I quickly sidestepped to keep from bowling her over.

"Welcome back," she said, assuming all was well. She sped up to walk alongside me.

"Thanks," I glibly replied, beginning to reflect on my memories of this place. People like her were a joy to work beside.

"Some woman has been calling repeatedly. Left messages for you, but I've been holding on to them. I think it's personal," she whispered.

I took the messages from her, already knowing who it was, but continued my pace toward Jacobi's office door without saying anything.

"Did I do okay? Jacobi said not to bother you with them."

When I reached the door to Jacobi's office, I glanced back. "Jacobi's not always someone to rely on. Remember that," I coldly offered. "It's been nice working with you."

"Um . . . and you too," she replied, stumbling for words before realizing it best to head back to her desk.

I grasped the door handle and barged in. Jacobi was on his phone, but the paralegal Sally—whom he referred to as incompetent—was beside him.

Behind his desk.

Unique way of training my permanent replacement.

Good ole Jacobi. Always good for the hands-on approach.

"Bro! I am so happy to see you," Jacobi said with a polished smile of his, pretending I hadn't startled him. Without saying good-bye, he ended his call and stood up. When he did that, he noticed the unsigned agreement in my hand. He nervously tried to smooth the wrinkles out on his shirt. Sally saw the look in my eyes, probably sensing this wasn't going to be professional, and quickly removed herself from his proximity.

"Sally, can you leave us—"

"I think she already got that message, man," I said, cutting him off.

"I—I'll talk to you later, Jacobi. It's good seeing you again, Chase."

She wasn't worth an answer at the moment. I was too focused on the snake in front of me lest I get bit. As Jacobi's door closed shut, I couldn't hold back any longer.

"I fuckin' trusted you, man!" I screamed. "And they've got me in there to sign papers based off your lies!"

"Wha—hold up, dude," he said, waving his hands as if directing traffic.

I leapt over the desk, tackling Jacobi full force. My first punch met my former friend's face square in the nose, blood erupting on call. The second and the third weren't far off. By that time I think he'd caught on. He rolled away from me, shielding his face as he tried to kick me off. I clubbed him across his back several times before he shoved his chair between us to allow him a brief respite. As he clambered to his feet, I yanked his phone off his desk and hurled it at his head. The edge struck him in the eye, sending him yelping in pain like a dog.

"What the fuck!" he said, wiping the blood from multiple sources on his face and looking at the crimson streak on his hand through a squinted eye. In that moment, he snapped as well. He shot at me with a looping overhand right, which I ducked under. As he tried to correct himself, I let it rip with a solid counterpunch to the jaw.

Jacobi succumbed to the blow, falling backward, where he landed with a flop on his butt. The office wall, with his framed diplomas, kept him from sprawling onto his back. Several frames fell off the wall from the thud, crashing on or around him with a cascade of glass.

He was ripe to be stomped down right about now, but I refrained. Only then did I notice the stinging scrape on my chin from one of his wild kicks.

"You lied about me to the partners? To save your neck?" I exclaimed while trying to catch my breath. "*And you said to trust you*? Like you were my friend? You're the one who can't keep his dick in his pants around here, man."

Jacobi chuckled through his swollen face, not bothering with defending himself any longer. "At least I don't come up with elaborate fantasies to justify fucking a beautiful woman. Be a fucking man for once," he gasped, trying to muster some smugness. I reconsidered stomping him.

"Why? Why, man? As much as I've done for you? Hell, even back in law school. You're supposed to be my boy. Why?"

"Because I need this job. I need it more than you, Chase. You're just here because Dawn approves, hoping you'll rethink taking the bar. And you can't even get that right."

"Don't you dare talk about me and my wife. That business is certainly none of yours."

"Why not? You're in my guest bedroom, ain'tcha? She kicked your ass out because you couldn't handle your business. If that was mine, I'd have that pussy under control, not having some imaginary crisis over some side chick. Besides, what makes you think Dawn's not getting it somewhere else while you play with this *soul mate* bullshit? You're a weak, directionless motherfucker."

A knock came at Jacobi's office door just as I was about to respond violently.

"Is everything okay in there?" a muffled voice asked from the hallway.

"Yeah. We're fine," Jacobi called out, summoning the energy to sound off. "Give us a minute."

"Damn. Dawn was right about you."

Jacobi laughed. "She was right about both of us."

I turned to leave, gifting the man who'd been my friend with a parting shot. "If Iris's husband files for divorce, the truth's going to come out about you and her around here anyway."

"No it won't," he responded as he tried to right himself from his predicament on the floor. "You're the one who slept with her. Just like I said. Her husband never caught us in the act. Only caught us hanging out at Hotel Zaza. If Iris divorces, at least she'll have me with a job as a lawyer . . . or maybe even partner. If she's claims I slept with her, I lose my job and we both have nothing. Like I said, I need this job. And all you had to do was sign the paper. We'd both have our jobs and it would be business as usual. A win-win. Now you're just S.O.L., shit out of luck."

"You devious, scheming bastard," I muttered, hand

on the door and preparing to leave his office and this place once and for all.

"Yep," he agreed with a big grin.

And on that note, I decided to stomp him after all.

34

"Get your hands off me!" I said, knowing they were about to release their grasp on my suit anyway. When the elevator opened, the two sport-coated men hastily pushed me across the lobby toward the revolving doors. Although my car was in the parking garage, building security threw me out onto Louisiana Street.

"Sir, don't think about returning," the one with a brown bushy moustache that concealed his entire top lip offered before leaving me outside with the rest of downtown Houston's foot traffic. As he walked away, he spoke into his radio to report on my situation.

Problem solved. The crazy, violent coworker who slept with the firm's client and beat down her husband as well as one of their attorneys would no longer bother them.

Thanks, Jacobi.

My suit jacket hung partially off a shoulder. Dried blood marred my shirt that now hung out of my pants like some sloppy kid. As I attempted to restore myself back to a presentable state, I heard ambulance sirens in the distance as they approached my former office building. Yeah, I'd lost my cool.

But it was worth it for that brief moment.

At least the firm hadn't called the police on me yet.

Walking to the garage to get my car, I called my mom on her cell.

"Well, my meeting is over," I exhaled.

"And? How did it go?" Earnestine asked.

"Enlightening," I replied.

"Is your leave over?"

"Oh, yeah. You might say that," I answered.

I was lost. No job and no home. So adrift aimlessly, I went in search of something that—as long as there was the slimmest of chances—I hadn't lost yet.

My mom begged for me to pass by her job so she could talk to me in person. Claimed she was worried about the stress I'd been under . . . and that it was too much. I would have to take the time to see her, though, and assure her I was okay.

I drove north up I-45 to the Woodlands, specifically the Woodlands Mall. More specifically, Macy's, where I drove around on the parking lot in search of Dawn's MINI Cooper. As a result of our blowup, she was working more hours.

I hadn't sent a batch of flowers to Dawn today. My plan was to deliver them myself with an invitation to dinner—a starting-over of sorts—after my first day back on the job. I told myself that the only difference was that I was going to arrive a bit earlier than originally planned.

Nothing like improvisation.

I also knew Dawn must be at work because she wasn't home. Against her wishes, I'd gone by there. Needed a change of clothes and a cleanup after what had occurred with Jacobi. Maybe more than that, I just wanted to be in my home. True to her word, she'd changed the front and rear door locks, but the alarm code was the same. Same for the garage door, which I used my car remote to open. After parking inside the garage, I kicked open the door to my house and quickly disarmed the alarm. Dawn would hate what I did, but I would fix it.

I would fix everything.

I just wanted to be home.

Clean, crisp, and composed, I left my car and entered Macy's with a dozen roses in hand. Going in the doors at the south entrance, an elderly woman in a tennis outfit complimented me on how nice the roses looked.

"Must be for a special someone," she said, a big smile forming behind her thick red lipstick.

"Yes, ma'am. They're for my wife. She works here."

"A surprise! Oh, how I love those," she gushed.

"I hope she does too," I replied with a nod as I entered the houseware and kitchen department.

I bypassed the escalators in the center of the store and made my way to the men's department, proudly holding the symbols of my love, devotion, and hopefully reconciliation. I found my wife by the cash register for urban apparel, where she was gathering clothes to be put back on the racks. She hadn't noticed me yet, deep in her work. I smiled to myself, having pictured this moment on my way here. Everything would be perfect with us back together.

I was ten feet away when that changed.

A young brother around six feet two swooped between us. All I could see of him was his ears and ill-fitting suit as his back obscured Dawn from my view. He was closer than I'd like. Close enough to brush up against Dawn's ass if he weren't careful.

If he wanted to be careful.

I slowed down, getting a better view of both them from the store walkway. He said something in Dawn's ear, to which she mumbled something in response. There was a light giggle and more relaxed body language between them. Dawn looked into his eyes for a moment, almost teasingly, before mumbling something else that I couldn't hear. When she resumed gathering clothes, my man put his hands on her shoulders and gave her a brief massage.

I was even with them now, wanting Dawn to shrug off the kid's hands or at least put some platonic distance between them. But she stayed put, even letting out a deep thankful sigh as his fingers worked her muscles.

"Dawn," I called out sternly.

Junior reacted first to seeing me glaring at him. He withdrew his hands almost faster than the eye could see, creating a faint breeze that I felt. By that time, Dawn had turned around toward the sound of my voice.

"Chase," she gasped. Much different sound than the one of joy she'd let out seconds ago. Hadn't realized that I'd lowered her flowers to my side by then, forming a death grip around them. Could just as easily be Junior's neck.

"I'll talk to you later," Junior offered as he backed up three full steps. Saw his name tag then. Said *Ronald* on it.

"Ronnie, this is my husband, Chase. Chase, this is my coworker Ronnie," she quickly rattled off, making sure titles, connections, and boundaries were established. I knew when she was blushing and Dawn was blushing now.

"Sup, bruh," I said, declining to relinquish my grip on her roses and shake his hand.

"Pleased to meet you, man," Ronnie of college age offered with a bit of restrained swagger. His false smile was full of teeth. Reminded me of Jacobi. Made me wonder if he looked at my wife with eyes like Jacobi while they worked together. Wondered if maybe he needed to be stomped too.

"Ronnie is one of our trainees," Dawn volunteered.

"Oh," was all I said as I dissected her with legal eyes, assessing her credibility and believability as if she were on the stand . . . or on an episode of *Maury*. Had got way too caught up on that shit while off work with nothing to do. *Dawn. When you said you didn't sleep with Ronnie the motherfuckin' trainee, the lie detector determined that was . . .*

"More flowers, Chase?" Dawn asked, breaking me from my afternoon TV episode just before Maury could read me the results. Didn't know if I'd be doing a happy dance, calling her a liar and a bleeped-out bitch while the audience booed her or if we'd make up and hug it out to a series of audience *aaawwwws*.

"Yeah," I replied. "Figured I'd bring them in person this time. Surprise you. *Surprise!*"

"Damn, you must've spent a whole paycheck on all these roses she's been getting," Ronnie spit out. She'd discussed my flowers with him? What else had she discussed? Was he a shoulder to cry on? Okay. I was tripping.

"Not even close," I replied. None of his business that I no longer had a job, but maybe a new set of charges on my credit card. "But my wife's worth it. Anything for Dawn."

Ronnie cut his eyes toward her, motioning that he was going find something to keep him busy in another part of the store. Good boy. "Nice meeting you," he offered as he departed from my space.

I nodded at him, waiting for several seconds before handing my wife her latest batch.

"What was that all about?" Dawn asked.

"You tell me," I shot back, regretting it as soon as it escaped my mouth.

"I'm training him. Put away your boxing gloves."

"If you say so."

"Look," she said. "Don't do this. Not at my job. I have nothing to be guilty about."

"I don't like him all up on you. And touching you."

"Relax. His dick ain't been in me. Can you say the same about yours, the rover?"

"I'm sorry. I deserve that. Just wanted to see you and ask you out to dinner. I miss you."

She smelled the roses, sighing to herself as she looked for somewhere to set them. "You didn't have to spend all this money. Especially with your job situation and the mortgage almost due."

"You know about work?"

"Yes. Your mother told me a little something. Said me you were under a lot of stress. Something to do with Jacobi?"

"Yes."

"Told you about him," she said, arms folding in an I-told-you-so stance.

"And you were right," I stated, deep down hoping this admission might open a door.

Speaking of doors.

"Hey. That shirt's from the house," she said, pointing at it as her eyes flared with fire. "How'd you get ahold of it?"

I exhaled, looking into her eyes. "I went home. Just for a moment. Only to change, that's all."

"But how did you get in? I changed the locks."

"Can we talk about that later?"

"*Did you break in?*"

"No. No. I came in through the garage. Don't worry. I disabled the alarm and I'm going to fix the door."

"Fix? So you did break in."

"How am I going to break into my own house, Dawn?" I offered, my voice raising in irritation before I caught myself. "Look . . . I didn't come here to argue. I just needed to change clothes before I came here. I wanted to make a good impression. I promise I'll fix the door. I came here to apologize again and ask you out to dinner.

Baby, I know I need to do more than this, but I want to make a fresh start. Let's go to Perry's Steakhouse tonight."

"Remember when we were supposed to go to Perry's last time? When you got in your car wreck?"

"Yeah," I replied.

"Were you with her that day?"

I said nothing, remembering coming to in the hospital with Ava at my side.

Dawn hesitated, shook her head, closed her eyes, then went back to work. "Just go. It's too much. Too soon, Chase."

I walked up to the old man sitting on a shopping cart. Dropped a five in his tip cup and sat down next to him. He eyed me strangely before trying to blast a note with that semi-healed lip of his. Several bucks and some change were already in his tip cup. Must've been making do.

"You not leavin'?" Joell asked, lowering the trumpet from his mouth.

"No. Got nowhere to be," I replied simply with a defeated shoulder shrug.

35

"Chase?"

"Yeah?" I replied, not recognizing the number. I had to remember where I was, focusing on the popcorn textured ceiling as I adjusted my eyes to the surroundings. Place still smelled the same—lived in. Maybe some additional moisture left over from Hurricane Ike. Bedroom definitely had more clutter than before I left for Sam Houston State. But Mom was nice enough to take me in while I plotted my next move. Where had my life gone?

"It's Kelli Jo. Did I catch ya at a bad time?" she asked politely.

"Who?" I asked, shaking off the cobwebs and throwing off the covers. I could hear a bus or loud truck in the background, further making it hard to hear.

"*You know*," she stressed, a little louder this time. "Kelli Jo. From work. I used to work with you."

"Oh. Sorry. Didn't recognize the number and didn't expect to hear from any of y'all."

"I'm calling you from outside the building on my personal phone. They don't know I'm speaking to you. We were forbidden. Sorry you're no longer with us," she said, full of sympathy and reverence. Felt like a dead man at his own funeral.

"Thanks. I appreciate it. Going to miss you too. But why the call? What's up?"

"That gal. Charla something or the other. She called

again. I had to tell her you're no longer with the firm. Sorry. Apparently she didn't believe me because she showed up causin' a ruckus. We told her not to return, but I just thought you should know. She wants to get in touch with you bad. Must be important, but I don't want to pry."

I let out a deep, long sigh. Listened to Kelli Jo's background noise on the phone while staring at the floorboards beneath my feet. Dug deep not to hang up and seek shelter beneath the covers again.

"Well, I appreciate that, Kelli Jo. And I'm sorry for her bothering you. Sorry for a lot of things," I said as I fidgeted with a fingernail.

"Hey. I gotta run, but keep your head up and chin out, Chase. Most people around here don't believe that stuff about you."

"Thanks for that. I'll do my best," I said, ending our conversation.

My morning was off to a roaring start. No solace and no further sleep. I shuffled into the kitchen, getting the coffeepot to work. Once my cup of Community Coffee was ready, I put on some clothes and stepped onto my mom's porch.

A school bus, embossed with Houston Independent School District on its side, passed with a batch of students, probably en route to M.C. Williams Middle School over on Knox Street, as I looked over a wad of balled-up papers I'd retained. I took a sip of the strong blend and finally read the messages given to me previously by Kelli Jo on the day I terminated my employment. Ava, as I suspected.

Let's get this over with, I thought as I added *67 before dialing the number to block my number from the caller ID.

"Chase," Ava stated rather than asking on the first ring.

"Yeah," I said as I continued to watch the traffic on Montgomery. A rusted-out Chevy C10 pickup honked at me, to which I saluted with my cup. Didn't have this kind of activity outside my house with Dawn out in the Spring suburbs. "You've been trying to reach me?"

"They said you no longer work downtown. Are you okay?"

"No. I'm not. And I'm tired of people asking me if I am. What do you want, Ava?"

"I need to see you."

"I thought we came to an understanding outside the courthouse. I'm not of a mood to indulge shit at the moment. Just leave me alone."

"I can't. Look . . . I'm going to be leaving soon, but I want to share something with you before I do . . . and it's too late."

"Tell me over the phone. I can't trust myself around you. You know that. And I'm in a bad way right now. Things are dark."

"I really need to see you. Maybe it'll do both of us good. Just a moment of your time. Face-to-face. It'll change your life. Both of ours."

"And I said, no. Damn, girl!" I cursed, pacing back and forth across my mom's creaky porch.

"I could go by your house," Ava stated, a sudden coldness sneaking into her voice. "I know where you live."

"Now you're threatening me?" I asked, angered while seriously worried about what would happen if Dawn saw her again.

"No. Not trying to cause further problems like that. But I . . . I'm kinda in a bad way myself. Feeling emotional these days. Mood swings. Anger sometimes."

"Sounds like we're in the same boat."

"That's because we're linked."

"Don't go there again. I won't allow it."

"Okay. But maybe this will help both us. Get back to where we need to be." A fiend is good with that hit, but is right back in a worse state as soon as that euphoria fades. Ava was that temptation for me no matter how barren the landscape of my life.

"You don't give up, do you?" I said wearily.

"Not this time. I can't. Just let me see you. No touching. No kissing. No—"

"Okay. Okay. I get it. Five minutes. And whatever it is better be important."

"It is, baby," she replied. I could sense the sunshine in her voice whenever she spoke like that. Damn her and damn me more.

"A public place. Has to be. Five minutes. No more."

I walked across the grass toward the Water Wall Fountain on Post Oak next to the Galleria, wearing a gray hoodie and black jogging pants. Beneath my Houston Texans baseball cap, black lenses obscured any view of the equally dark bags beneath my tired eyes. Although a good spot for couples and tourists, the locals in the uptown area also gathered on nice days to picnic on the surrounding grounds or feel the cool mist off the well-known sculpture. For me, it was a decent public spot with no emotional attachment for either of us.

My mom had called from work to check on me. Told her I was fine. As far as she knew I was grabbing some lunch. I checked my watch, seeing I was punctual even with parking by Nordstrom and running over.

Beneath one of several oak trees, someone waved at me. She was closer to Post Oak and had maybe been dropped by cab there. Being less in view of prying eyes and with a little shade, I motioned for her to stay put as I approached. The brief walk across the park gave me a moment to get my head on straight before finding out what was so important for us to meet.

When I came closer, Ava stepped out from the shade of the oak tree.

"Hey, baby," she said, extending both hands for me to take them rather embracing me in a hug. Maybe my words had gotten through to her. But I was immediately surprised by a change in her appearance. Ava's hair was tucked beneath a colorful head scarf with just a few random strands breaking up the black Chanel shades that hid her eyes as well. She was covered in a loose-fitting white tunic with black capris and ornate flip-flop sandals. What surprised me was the fullness of her face as well as her feet, which appeared swollen. Also, a dash of acne had broken out across her cheeks and nose. For someone of who I had intimate knowledge, the sudden changes were puzzling. Still, I tried ignoring it. I wasn't here to check her out.

"Five minutes starts now," I uttered coolly. She still held my hands. Looked like we were about to break into a waltz.

"Chase. Please. Can't I just enjoy this?"

"Okay. Hi," I said, throwing a smile on before going blank- faced again. Ava giggled in response. She came closer, almost to embrace me, but stopped short. Part of me yearned for that proximity and felt cheated. But my life was too fractured to indulge it. Our fingers intertwined on instinct, though.

I shook my head at how foolish I was to come out here.

"I did have something to tell you. Just worried about how you'll react."

I slid my hands free, looking straight in her face; a face that seemed a little odd. "Oh my God. Did you give me an STD?" I asked, broaching the first thing that came to mind.

"No!" she chastised me. Then she bit her bottom lip, an odd grin surfacing. "But I am giving you something."

"Huh?"

"Are you blind, Chase?" she asked.

I removed my sunglasses, becoming accustomed to the glare, then began scrutinizing Ava more closely. Suddenly my world began to spin.

"I'm pregnant," she uttered just as the impossible began to register. The tunic was a maternity top. The fullness of her face made sense now. But . . .

"You're pregnant," I gasped.

"That's what I just said. Yes, Chase, I'm pregnant," she said, smiling.

"That's not what I mean," I spat out. "This doesn't make sense. You're far along, Ava. Too far. We just—"

"Calm down. I don't understand it, either," she said, allowing me to make out a definitive baby bump beneath her top. I placed my hands on her stomach and my eyes widened.

"No, no, no! I saw you just a few weeks ago at the gallery. When we—No. You didn't look like this. You weren't pregnant then. But now you're like several months along or something."

"I guess it has something to do with the differences in our worlds."

"Difference in what? What are you talking about?" I muttered, cutting my eyes at her. This had to be some kind of joke. A sick, cruel one, but a joke.

"Where I'm from," she offered, fumbling for an answer. "I've been trying to read up on this. Maybe time flows a little different."

"Stop. This isn't making sense. You're not from some other world, Ava. That's a bunch of crazy bullshit that you got me caught up in."

"But it's the truth. Look at me," she urged, presenting me with the basis for her argument.

"No it's not! And you can't be pregnant from me. Certainly not this far along. It isn't humanly possible."

"But I am. With your child. Our child."

I went to grasp her stomach once again, placing my hands under her top this time. Ava calmly looked up at me, smiling serenely as I tried to fathom what was going on. She placed her hands atop mine. It wasn't a pillow or some piece of special- effects makeup. It was flesh and I could feel a life kicking inside.

But how?

Oh my God.

Dawn.

"I had to see you, Chase. Do you understand now? We'll be together forever. Our child . . . our child will link us forever."

I pulled my hands off her and began backing away.

"Ava, I gotta go. I gotta figure this out," I voiced. Backpedaling as I tried to wrap concepts and notions completely alien to me around in my fatigued head.

"Chase no!" Ava screamed. I didn't understand her tone. I just knew I needed to get away from here. And her screaming wouldn't stop me.

But in my haste, I had backed off the sidewalk and into the street.

Where a speeding taxicab on Post Oak struck me.

She was trying to warn me.

36

I came to, riding a wave of confusion and nausea.

As well as the inability to move my right arm.

Ouch.

It was in a sling and encased in a cast. I began to panic and tried to sit up. But I ached badly. Could feel bruises all over my body beneath the thin gown.

"Take it easy," she said. A soft voice of comfort as her hand rested on my arm—the good one.

At Ben Taub General Hospital. Thoughts jumbled. It was nighttime now. I think I'd been here a long time. From my perspective, a marathon of bright overhead lights, ceiling tiles, and doctors talking. And she was here. Just like last time I was in a hospital. At my bedside.

Ava.

But now Ava was pregnant. Way pregnant.

It was as if dunking my face in ice water.

I remembered how I got here.

"What did you say, Chase?"

"Huh?" I groaned. I was afraid of what I may have said without knowing.

"Do you understand me?" Dawn asked. Dawn my wife. Not Ava, the mother of my unborn child.

No. I imagined that. She couldn't be pregnant. At least not that far along.

But if I did imagine things, what was I doing here in the hospital?

I gazed at Dawn and smiled. She'd come down here to be at my side. Nothing else seemed to matter.

"They called me. I was home," she offered to my un-asked question and perhaps false hopes.

"They worry that you tried to kill yourself."

"No, no, I—I was backing up. I must've slipped," I mumbled, my voice cracking as I went to speak louder.

"Into the street? In front of a moving car? You were by the Galleria, Chase. You mother doesn't even know what you were doing there. This doesn't make sense," Dawn proposed. She closed her eyes and pinched the bridge of her nose, her way of facing the onset of a stress headache.

How could I tell her I got Ava pregnant? And if I dared mention the circumstances or what I saw, they would be sure to commit me. If I couldn't trust my mind and my own eyes, how could I trust my actions?

"What'd the doctor say?" I asked, giving up on trying to reason away my actions with Dawn.

"Broken arm, concussion, bruising, and some muscle sprains or strains. You're lucky. Very. They're waiting on results from your CT scan. Just to ensure you don't have a closed head injury."

"Is my mom here?"

"Yes. She's speaking with the doctors. She brought somebody with her. I'll go get them."

"Wait. Stay with me," I said, snagging her wrist be-fore she could leave. She still had trouble looking at me.

"Chase. Don't do this. I came because I was concerned, but don't read anything beyond that." Dawn gently re-moved my hand and placed it back on my chest.

"Do you still love me?" I asked as I tried to sit up again. This time, with effort, I was able to right myself in the hospital bed.

"I feel like I don't know you anymore. The better question is, *Do you love yourself?* If so, get some help and we can revisit this. Much later. Maybe. Now, just rest and I'll go get them."

When Dawn said *them,* I wondered who'd accompanied my mom. If it was Ava, I didn't know how I'd react. Where had she'd gone, anyway? Had she stayed by my side to the hospital like last time? Or did she figure she'd do me a favor and get ghost when the ambulance took off?

One of my myriad questions was answered when my mom entered the room with my dad in tow behind her. I guess Dawn wasn't sure how I'd react if she'd told me. Joell wore a clean shirt for a change and was moderately presentable—my mom's handiwork, no doubt. For him to travel this far without pitching a fit was a miracle. I tried to look alert and comfortable for them.

"I hope you got my clothes so I can get out of here," I uttered merrily.

"They want to keep you for observation, Chase. Worry you might have a head injury. The doctor will be in here in a little bit to talk to you," my mom stated. She never called me by my birth name. *Boy* held more love on most days. "What's going on with you, boy? You fightin' everyone, you losin' yo job, you sleepin' around—"

"Mom, it's not like—"

"Be quiet, I'm talking!" Earnestine roared, continuing her diatribe. "You was supposed to be getting some lunch. Not stepping out in front of cabs! Boy, now you got people worried you tryin' to commit suicide. If all this is a cry for help, we listening, baby. Me and your daddy. We both listenin'."

Seeing my mom full of so much passion and concern hurt when it should've been touching. It hurt because she should know me better than to believe I was intentionally deconstructing my life. Thing is . . . I couldn't tell her the truth.

Because even I was lost when it came to that.

"I'm sorry, Mom," I whispered, breaking down and shedding tears over the grief I was causing her. She came closer, cradling my head on her chest.

"It's okay. We'll get you the help you need," she cooed.

Help? No! Nothing was wrong with me. Sure I'd been erratic . . . but Ava brought it out in me.

Ava, who claimed she was—

"I think I just need to get away for a little while. I'm too close to my problems. Need to go to Austin or something for a week. Come back recharged. Can you see about getting me checked out?" I restrained myself from grimacing over the constant throbbing behind my eyes.

"They gonna probably want you to stay overnight . . . at least, but I'll go find the doctor. There was a shooting on Harwin, so they're kinda busy tonight."

As my mom left, I eyed my clothes in a neat little stack on the chair beside the bed. My dad remained in the room, clinging close to the wall. This was straining him. Both his hands stayed in front of him, clasping that damn trumpet of his. He kept his head bowed.

I lowered the railing and kicked one leg over the side of the bed, gauging whether I could walk.

"They think you're like me," Joell grunted, pointing to his head and whatever imaginary beasts roamed inside it.

"I'm not," I remarked. "Stuff's been rough, though. I went down a path that I gotta see through to the end now. Things have taken an unexpected turn. "

"Overheard your momma talkin' 'bout you and some woman. A lot like me," he said, this time pointing downward on his body.

"Not if I can help it," I scoffed. "This was different. A woman told me things . . . taught me things. About myself. It's like they're not true, but they could be. You probably don't know what I'm talking about. Did you know . . . I can play the piano?"

"Yeah. I know, boy," he said, acknowledging me with his eyes for the first time tonight.

"How?"

"Because I'm the one who sat you down at the piano. A little bar off Shepherd where my band used to play. They weren't supposed to let you in, but . . . You were good too."

I lowered my other leg onto the floor, startled by my dad's revelation as I tried to find my balance. "I don't remember any of that," I stated.

"You were little still. Tiny little thing. I could tell, though. I wonder about that. How different stuff mighta been if I'd stayed around."

"Maybe I'd be famous like you," I joked, hearing a certain woman's voice in my head. A voice with fanciful tales I blew off.

"Fame ain't nothin' without family," Joell grunted.

Family.

"Dad, there's something I need to do. I gotta get out of here. Now. Will you help me?" I asked.

Joell Hidalgo found the courage to step away from the wall on which he'd been leaning. He released his hold on his trumpet and came forward, moving into the center of the room.

A solitary nod was all he gave me.

37

"Wait right here," I said to the cabbie. It had taken his assistance to exit the van. With my arm in a sling, I draped my hoodie over my shoulders and limped into the Walgreens at the corner of Fannin and North Macgregor. Just down the block from Ben Taub General, where my dad had helped me dress and sneak into the elevator. To go along with whatever treatment plans the doctors had prescribed would only slow me down. I had no time to be sidelined.

With Ava talking about leaving town, I needed the truth now.

And I'd learned, working in my profession all these years, is that sometimes to get at the truth, you need a lie.

Or rather a liar.

I grabbed several bottles of extra-strength Motrin, a box of Epsom salt ,and some ice packs off the shelf, dialing a number on my phone that fared better than my body.

"Surprised you'd want to talk to me. Calling to apologize? Or to beg for a reference?"

"Hell no," I said, grimacing as I limped toward the refrigerated section for a bottle of cherry Pepsi. Had to stop and lean against a store endcap filled with Snuggies on display for a moment.

"You sound like death."

"Sorry to disappoint you, but I still live. Need a favor from you."

"Go fuck yourself," Jacobi replied. I was only a mile or two from his place. If in better shape, I would've considered showing up to argue my case in person.

"You did a good enough job of that at Casey Warner."

"You deserved what you got, you unappreciative bastard."

"I didn't call for niceties. But how's your face, by the way?" I asked, mustering a spiteful chuckle that hurt my sore ribs. The ringing in my head was still present.

"I'm about to hang up. I'm only giving you these seconds because you were my boy once."

"I need records. Fast. And you can get them for me," I said

"Can't help you."

"You will."

"Or what? Gonna beat me up again? You caught me in my work mode when you chose to go gangsta. I'm ready for you this time."

"You and what security, bitch?"

"Good one. But you see I had the last laugh. Now you're on the phone begging me for something."

"I'm not begging, but I will say please. I really need this, man."

"Must be important for you to semi-beg. Still, don't see how you're gonna make me do your bidding. Goodbye—"

"Wells Fargo," I said calmly. "I was with you at Casey Warner long enough to know what is a fuckup on your part and what is intentional. I know about your rainy-day fund at Wells Fargo and how you divert false expenditures into it. You still have dreams of making partner? Well, you can't put that one on me if they were to find out."

"You can't prove that shit."

"Don't have to. Bet the partners could. Last time I checked, Casey Warner hadn't changed their number."

"I'm listening," he growled, simmering on the other end of the phone call. I smiled, happy with my bluff. He'd only proven what I suspected.

"I need medical records, specific case files from a Dr. Charla Prisbani," I requested, reciting the name I'd seen on Ava's prescription bottles. "She's a psychiatrist."

"*If* I were to do this, where is she located?"

"I know she practices here in Houston. Find her. Get this for me and I'll forget any potential stories I might have about you and your illustrious career."

"This is about that damn girl, huh? And all these years, I thought we were friends."

"If we were still friends, I wouldn't be asking this of you. But you took care of that. Just get it for me."

"How? With my good looks?"

I sighed, beginning to walk again. "I don't work there and you're still having me figuring things out for you. Forge a subpoena using one of your existing cases. One that will scare her office into coughing it up on the spot when you present it. You're smooth. I trust you'll get it done and get me what I need. Time is of the essence. I'll give you until tomorrow afternoon."

"Blackmail and extortion is a crime. You do remember that, right?"

"I'm that desperate. Consider it a compliment that I would trust your talents and ask you."

I had Jacobi take down the information I had on Ava to better allow him to forge a subpoena. The federal privacy laws would make this a difficult one, but if Dr. Prisbani were a straight or bi female, Jacobi should be able to get the job done.

After paying for my quick first aid, I checked my phone. Missed calls were pouring in from my mom, even one from Dawn that gave me pause. As much as I wanted to, I couldn't call them back yet. They'd live.

I entered the cab, telling him to just drive. I needed time to think. Someone else needed to know I was okay. Looking at Reliant Stadium as we passed on I-610, I decided to reach out.

"Chase! Oh, thank God!" Ava squealed. "It's so good to hear your voice. I didn't mean to startle you with my condition. When I saw that car coming toward you, I thought I'd lost you. You're lucky it hit its brakes and swerved."

"Yeah," I said. "I think I remember sticking my arm out in front of me when I saw it. But that's it. What happened next?"

"After you took a spill, I stayed by your side until the ambulance came. I gave them your name and information, but didn't want to create more problems for you with your family, so I stayed behind. That was hard to do. Are you still in the hospital?"

"Yeah," I answered, thinking it through.

"How bad off are you, love?"

"I'm okay. Just some bumps," I replied, to which the cabbie looked in his rearview mirror and frowned. "Sorry to scare you. Is the baby okay?" Felt wrong saying it, but I had to acknowledge what I saw. What I felt.

"Yes. Thank you for asking," she said warmly. "I don't know whether to say *him* or *her*. This . . . this is startling for me too. I should see a doctor. It really hurts sometimes. And as fast as this is going, it won't be much longer."

"Maybe I can see the two of you . . . again. When I get released. It'll be soon."

"Good. That would be nice. Like I said. I'll be leaving soon. Going back home."

"Back to Louisiana? Pouppeville, right? That shouldn't be too long a drive."

" . . . I suppose," Ava said after a long pause.

Again with not understanding her.

Next time I saw her, I would have my answers.

I ripped open the packaging and popped the top on the Motrin with my good hand. Downing a couple of tablets with some Pepsi, I sought a little relief from the pain I was in.

"Hey. I just took my meds, so I'm going to have to call you back tomorrow."

"I understand. Sleep tight. Be sure to listen to the nurses."

"I will," I replied, wishing I was being cared for by trained professionals.

Ending my conversation with Ava, I called out for the cabdriver to find me a hotel downtown.

Soon. Very soon.

I'd been sitting in the Ragin' Cajun restaurant in the downtown tunnels not far from Casey, Warner & Associates. Left my hotel and got here early so as to enjoy a bowl of chicken and shrimp gumbo and take a seat before his arrival.

As the lunchtime crowd diminished, returning to their offices in the towering spires in the bright Texas sun aboveground, I remained seated. I checked my watch, anticipating the lull. Jacobi arrived as I read from a copy of the *Houston Defender*. The man had been sweating and looked downright off his game. Amazing how much my threat had done to motivate him.

"Here," he said, flipping a large brown envelope atop my newspaper. I looked up from my read, trying to be discreet.

"Is that it?"

"No, is *that* it?" he retorted, hoping to be done with me I'm sure. "Whoa, you look sick."

Ignoring Jacobi's statement about my appearance, I took the envelope in my hand. The heft felt right for a file. I kept my cast below the table and my jacket covering the sling. No need him knowing. Might try to sneak me with a punch. "You really did it," I said.

"You're not going to open it?"

"Not here," I said, not wanting him to see me struggle with a lone hand. "If it's not, then it's *not it*."

"You don't know what I had to do for that," he muttered, leaning over the table with a false smile for only me to hear.

"Had trouble drafting the subpoena?" I taunted.

"No. I didn't do that shit. You know I've never been good at that kind of stuff. That—that's what you were around there for. To make things work. Until you went and fucked things up," he said, his voice growing distant at the end. A hint of regret? If I believed him capable of it.

"Then how did you—"

"I got what you wanted. Had other things planned for this morning already, so I acquired it last night."

"Last night? A break-in? Did anyone get hurt?"

"No. But somebody had to be paid for the job. We're straight, right?"

"Yeah. We're good. Thank you," I politely offered to him, potential future partner with Casey, Warner & Associates.

"I never saw you. I never spoke to you. I never want to see you again," he responded with his parting shot. Then he abruptly turned his back to me and exited the restaurant, entering the flow of foot traffic outside to disappear again—a suit among a human river of suits.

I couldn't get up fast enough to return to my hotel room and see what the file held.

38

"Boy, where are you?" Earnestine yelled as I finally answered her call. "If you're tryin' to convince me that you're not out your ever-lovin' mind, you're failin' miserably!"

"I'm okay, Mom," I said, closing the hotel curtains. Light had begun making the headache worse.

"Okay? The hospital went into a panic when you disappeared. They don't like what they saw in your CT scan results. Need you to come back for further tests. And how the hell did you get dressed? Did Joell help you? I will beat his crazy, foolish ass."

"No, Mom. You know he's not capable of that," I countered, protecting the elder Hidalgo. "I'm just not as bad as they thought. How else could I walk out of there? Didn't mean to scare you. Have some business I need to handle. And I'm not losing my mind."

"Do you love your wife?" my mom asked sharply.

"Of course. What kind of question is that?" I replied as I reached over and turned on the desk lamp.

"Then you need to stop this foolishness. She thinks all of this is because of that artist woman. Whatever chance you have is slipping away. For good."

"That's what I'm trying to do now. Make sense of it all. Look. I gotta go. Tell Dawn that I love her," I remarked as I upended the envelope, spilling its contents onto the desk.

If Jacobi really had someone break into the psychia-

trist's office, this stuff was hotter than I'd like if they
noticed it missing. And if somebody had been hurt, I
couldn't undo that. But I'd asked for it. No balking at
the method in the aftermath.

I spread the documents out and sifted through them.
Wanting to understand what I was poring over from top
to bottom. A microcassette was included in an envelope,
but I didn't have anything to play it on.

Over the next hour or so, I tried to make sense of
Dr. Prisbani's handwritten notes and typed session sum-
maries, forming a mental picture of Ava from her perspective. Certain details came alive for me despite it becoming increasingly hard to concentrate.

*Found in the bathroom of a couple's home in the
Heights.

* Arrested for trespassing, but unknown how she got
in. Claimed to be owner of the house and that couple were
somehow trespassers. Disoriented and confused.

* Taken into custody. Unable to present ID.

* No record of her in the system.

*Not even fingerprints or Social Security number on
file.

*Referred for additional evaluation upon release from
hospital observation. Receiving assistance from Smith
Sampson with acclimation and basic living arrange-
ments.

*Says her name is Ava. Claims to be from a town in
Louisiana called Pouppeville. Unable to locate such a
place.

*Subject is a fascinating individual. Well educated and
expressive. Took particular interest based on complex
fantasies where even I have trouble not believing.

*In her imagined world, a lot is the same as the real
world. Minor differences in architecture, cars, boats
and planes, but some distinct differences. Past—Unit-

ed States has fifty-two states; Puerto Rico and Cuba added in the 1960s. Malcolm X and Bobby Kennedy survived assassination attempts. Recent—Al Gore won in a narrow election, serving two terms. 9-11 didn't happen as well as Iraq War. Before her "coming here," Republican John McCain held a commanding lead in general election polls over Democrat nominee John Edwards once details of Edward's affair surfaced.

* Has crafted a parallel world for herself, worthy of a novel. However, this fantasy of hers is pathological; a defense in coping with loss.

*Shows immense artistic ability. Claims she was a renowned artist where she came from. Now paints to cope with loss of her husband and her home. Husband was famous pianist. College sweethearts at SHSU.

*In mourning as husband died in a random traffic accident while touring in the Netherlands. Wasn't with him. Was supposed to go, but had minor disagreement. Doesn't forgive herself. Feels she's here in "our world" either as punishment or second chance. Thinks punishment.

*Irrational fixation on her deceased husband. Probable guilt. Helping her with coping strategies and how to move on.

*Worry what might happen if she meets someone she thinks is this man Chase. Could be major setback in mental state with dire consequences.

And I came along. Outside a pub one night.

"Lord no," I gasped.

39

I stood up from the desk, feeling a bit warm. Probably just nerves and exhaustion. Of course, what I'd read of the psychiatrist's notes should've put me on my ass alone.

If Dr. Prisbani had seen Ava's stomach—touched it like I had and felt the life growing inside, I wonder if her clinical opinion would change. Maybe I should call her. Get her to see Ava and provide me with a second opinion. To tell me I wasn't alone in thinking Ava was something greater than we, in our tiny focused lives, could imagine. To make me feel I was still sane.

But that would involve me admitting I'd had her patient records stolen.

The pain in my head worsened, making my eyes tear up. I limped toward the table and poured myself a glass of water over ice. I was already on my second bottle of Motrin, quickly downing six of them with several gulps of water. I'd be better. Now I had to get out of here. See Ava. Tell her I know.

That I believed her.

But first . . . I was so tired. Had pushed myself too hard. Needed to sleep. Just a quick catnap and I'd bounce back.

I fixed my smarting eyes on the bed in front of me. After resting the cool drinking glass against my forehead, I wandered over and collapsed atop the comforter.

Just . . . a . . . little . . . nap.

"Ahhh!" I yelped, sitting up too quickly. Arm itched like hell with the cast. Still had no idea how bad the fracture was or what kind of break. But it was my spiking headache that bothered me more.

What time was it? *Get it together, Chase,* I thought to myself.

It was nighttime, light no longer threatening to aggravate my sensitive eyes. The constant of downtown activity just beyond the windows had subsided too.

"Oh, shit," I blurted out. Was it even the same day? It wasn't the headache that awakened me, rather the persistent buzzing of my phone. I wondered how long and how often it had been doing that. I saw the number and quickly answered.

"Ava," I called out, frowning over the case of cotton mouth I was experiencing. The ice in my glass had melted too.

"Chase . . . Can—hear me?" I heard her voice say over the bad connection.

"Yes. I can hear you. But you're spotty," I replied. "I—I need to talk to you. I need to come over. Okay?"

"Hurry. I—"

"Ava! What? Say it again."

"—have to go. It's time, Chase."

"Time? Time for what? Can you hear me? Ava!" I yelled into the phone. Like it would do any good. As fast as this pregnancy was progressing, was she about to give birth? On a normal day, I couldn't tell the difference between trimesters, but whatever was happening to Ava defied any normal calculations.

Oh my God. I was going to be a father.

What if this accelerated growth resulted in a deformity?

Or worse?

Death.

I felt flush, needing some water right away to keep from passing out. I pushed myself to my feet on the strength of my good arm and swiftly moved to the table. While trying to listen beyond the whirring static, I filled my glass and downed another few Motrin. But as bad as I felt, Ava had to be worse.

"—I can feel it," came through clearly during a break in the interference that kept rolling in every few seconds. Shit. These phones were supposed to be the best.

"Hold up! Feel what, Ava? Contractions? Is that what you are saying? Listen, we need to get you to the hospital. Okay?"

" . . . love . . . you."

"I—I—listen. I love you too," I uttered, finally giving in the overwhelming tide, no longer fearful of it or its crushing weight. Felt liberating. "Are you there? Ava? Ava!"

"There's a pregnant woman inside. Wait here," I instructed the cabdriver as I awkwardly exited and hobbled up the steps to Ava's door. En route here, she'd quit answering her phone, stoking my fears. Adrenaline carried me as I beat on the door over and over.

"Ava, can you hear me?" I yelled to no response. When I grabbed the door handle, I realized it was unlocked.

As quickly as I could, I made my way through her home. Checked every room, every corner, every space possible.

But she was nowhere to be found.

Not even in her sanctuary where she healed herself, casting reminders of home in oils and watercolors atop canvass.

And where I played notes to Tupac for her.

Tupac . . . the mayor of Oakland, she'd said. Didn't quite feel so silly now.

The piano in the corner was uncovered. A hastily torn sheet of yellow notepad paper sat atop the keys. I went over, picked it up, turned it over, and read from it. Expected the name of the hospital to which she'd gone so I could run out of here and instruct the cabdriver to get me there pronto.

No.

That wasn't to be.

Chase,

Going home, my love.

Can fight it no longer.

Thank you for all you've given me in our short time reunited.

For you are always . . . my <u>happiness</u>.

Ava.

I screamed aloud, my weary, beaten mind considering that what Ava had left me was a suicide note. I lost all control, running through her place, yelling out her name as I looked for some trace—some clue—that perhaps she could still be found. In her bedroom, I found her purse.

And her phone.

Either she departed in such a hurry that she left them. Or she had no further use for them.

Had no intention of coming back.

When I emerged from her place, I was as if a madman. There was no sign of Ava in either direction. The cabdriver raised his hands off the steering wheel, waiting for his next set of directions. As long as his meter was running, he didn't care.

But I did.

And the pain in my heart rose up to surpass anything my failing body had endured. I grabbed the railing to steady myself as I slowly descended.

"My friend, do you want me to take you back home?" the driver asked when I got to him.

Home.

With that singular thought, another bolt of shooting pain rang through my head. I braced myself on the cab.

"You don't look well, my friend. Maybe you go to hospital? Maybe you come back later?"

I opened my eyes, beginning to respond and saw Ava's file, which I'd left on the backseat.

"No," I replied. "I know where we need to go."

40

I had the cab take me to the Heights, not knowing if I was right. Inside the envelope, among the papers to which I hadn't paid much attention, was an address on Nicholson Street.

The address of the couple where Ava first showed up.

The place Ava claimed was her home and not theirs.

My cab driver, a thin little man named Baku, knew how best to get there, taking I-45 north to I-10 west followed by hasty exit onto North Shepherd, which is where we were now.

"Are you okay back there, my man?" he asked, splitting his vision between looking for Dorothy Street and monitoring my condition in the rearview mirror.

"Go. Just go," I instructed. It seemed the closer we came to this address in the psych file, the more unbearable the daggers in my skull became. I quit talking, speaking only when I had to, so as to stave it off. Maybe it wasn't the location, but the woman I sought who was triggering this intense reaction in me. Only fitting that other irrational actions were triggered when in her presence. Maybe this was the culmination . . . a reversal of our attraction.

Where she was making me sick.

Literally.

Finding Dorothy Street, Baku slowed just enough to make the turn without knocking me around too much. We sped by Lawrence Park, then zigged onto West Eighth

Street, picking up speed. I clenched my teeth and tried to focus beyond my discomfort.

My anticipation grew as we edged the two blocks up Nicholson, looking for the right address. If Ava wasn't here, I was lost. But I knew she and the baby were.

The hairs on the back of my neck were speaking to me through the pain. The same electricity from that night outside the pub.

"Stop," I called out with eyes closed.

"Are you sure?" my driver asked.

I opened my eyes to see a two-story traditional home in chocolate with ivory trim. The front gate was askew and a **FOR SALE** sign was posted in the tiny front yard. Per the psych report, Ava had claimed it was hers and not the couple's.

Now she could claim sole possession. For a fairly new home, this wasn't much of a surprise in neighborhoods around Houston these days. People who were overextended were forced to make tough choices.

I handed my cabbie his fare plus another twenty.

"That's very generous of you, sir," he said with an appreciative smile. "Need me to stay?"

"No. You've been very helpful, but I'll take it from here," I replied as I opened the cab door.

"I don't think there's anybody there," Baku said as he craned his neck in the direction of the house we were parked in front of.

"Somebody's there," I stated before I shut the door and patted on the roof for him to be off.

A wave of nausea overcame me as I entered the gate. Could've sworn I felt the ground move beneath me too.

Exhaustion.

Exhaustion and the injuries I'd ignored until now.

Steadying myself, I walked onto the porch and peered into the front window. Saw nothing and the front door was still locked. But the hairs on my neck were taut as wires. I tried desperately to test the door, but it won. Excruciating pain now shot through my broken arm from trying to be a hero. I stepped down off the porch and tried to look around back. There was only the tiniest of spaces between the home and the fence that divided the properties, but I shoved myself along the side, banging my knees as I inched toward the rear.

Several minutes passed before I emerged, dirty and scratched up, to free myself. I climbed onto the back deck and looked inside the kitchen. The French doors had been busted open with a large ceramic pot that now rested on the hardwood floors just inside. I entered, following Ava's presumed path as tiny bits of broken glass shifted and cracked beneath my feet.

"Ava!" I called out as I tried to listen for some sign of life in the vacant, staged property. Nobody replied. Just as I did at her place, I went from room to room. On the first floor there was nothing to be found, but darkness. At least the streetlights kept me from crashing into walls. That left the second floor.

I carefully ascended the stairwell, keeping my back to the wall and extending my free hand into the darkness. But I could see my hand. There was power upstairs: A low light that bathed the upper hallway. Another wave of nausea overtook me when I reached the landing.

"Ava!" I yelled again as I wiped the sweat from my forehead and pressed on. I found a light switch and flipped it up. The darkness remained unchanged. Shaking my head, I continued down the hallway where the glow emanated from under a bathroom door. This time, I knew for certain I felt a vibration as I got closer. But with no power, what was causing it?

"Chase," I heard in a muffled gasp from behind that door. I took off running toward it. Like the front, this door was locked too.

"Ava, open the door! It's me!" I called out, banging frantically. Another sharp wave of pain ripped through my body, but I ignored it as best I could. "Where is that light coming from? Do you have a candle?"

"Chase . . . I don't want you to get hurt."

"Let me in, dammit! You—you're not gonna hurt me. Is something wrong with our baby?"

"No. Nothing wrong," she answered whimsically. Wondered if she was delirious . . . or had overdosed on something. "Our baby is going to be fine, Chase. I promise you."

I kicked at the door in frustration, but it wouldn't budge. I foolishly threw my hurt shoulder into it next and bounced off. I spilled onto the hardwood floor, writhing in pain from my serious mistake. It was as if running into a solid wall. "Whatever you're doing in there, stop. Please. I read your file. I believe you."

"I knew you would eventually, my love. But it's too late. It's time to go."

"No! It's not. Just open the door. Come out and talk to me. Please. I read your note. It—it doesn't have to end."

"It's beyond my control, Chase. I knew my time here was limited. Just didn't know when it would end. Wish it weren't tonight, but it is."

"End? No, no, no!" I howled, getting back to my feet. Felt more wobbly than before. Sweat had formed on my nose. When I wiped it, I realized it was blood. What the fuck? Didn't matter right now, but whatever was taking place beyond the door was affecting me. "Open the door, Ava! Don't do this! I'm begging you!" I urged while pounding with my fists. The light beneath the door ebbed and flowed now, almost like a pulse. A countdown toward something that couldn't be good.

"Why, Chase? You have your wife here. You've made it very apparent where I stand in your life," she called out through the door. Her voice sounded like she was in distress; the baby growing in spurts again, perhaps.

"That was then. I tried. Hell, I'm still trying. I—I just can't say what's going to happen tomorrow."

"*Who knows tomorrow's plans for you,*" Ava remarked with a sigh.

That was it. This had to end. I switched from pleading to ordering. "Don't you dare do anything to yourself or our baby! Do you hear me? I love you!"

I heard her gasp in pain. "I'm sorry, Chase," she called out. Whatever was taking place in that bathroom kicked up a notch. Felt like static cling all over me this time, miles beyond that intoxicating vibe from our first meeting. Even my watch was throwing off sparks, causing me to yank it off my wrist in a panic. This one couldn't be explained away as emotion, hormones or lust. It was a physical manifestation that was steadily building. Blood from my nose was now spotting my shirt as the light beneath the door grew in intensity as if alive itself. I needed to get in there and stop her.

Couldn't live without her.

I went back to the stairwell to gather myself for a running start. From a distance, it seemed like the bathroom was on fire, burning from the inside with an otherworldly flame. Some of this light had to be escaping, providing a light show outside for the neighbors to notice. I sprinted down the hall, covering half the distance in seconds as I prepared to become a human battering ram against a door that felt as immovable as a stone block.

Before I could make contact with the door, a blast of energy erupted from behind it, dispersing outward and bathing everything in its path. I crumpled, suddenly robbed of all momentum as an invisible wave struck me. With only one free hand I slammed into the floor, face-first. Like a marionette whose strings had been cut, I fell in an unceremonious heap. As I lay there, pain engulfed me to the point where I almost wanted to end my own life. Still, I dragged myself the rest of the way, coming to the unyielding door again and placing my hand upon it.

"*Ava!*" I called out a final time before relenting to the unforgiving punishment beyond my comprehension.

Then it was over.

The light show and whatever else was happening behind the door had ceased.

Only my ragged breathing remained to tell me my life was spared.

Darkness reigned again in the house on Nicholson Street. I laid still, trying to regain my composure. There were no sounds of life in the bathroom.

"Ava, what did you do?" I whispered to myself. Just then, a thunderous boom came from downstairs. It was the front door. As flashlight beams bounced wildly off the walls and ceilings in their search, I tried to get back to my feet. I'd propped myself against the hallway wall when the beams of light converged on me. Sounded like a large fire engine had just arrived outside.

"Freeze! Police! Put your hands up and don't move!" said one of the shadowy figures coming up the stairs. I raised the only free arm I had, tensing in that I might get tazed or shot if they failed to recognize the cast on the other one. Two of the figures branched off and nabbed me. For all my effort to stand, I was rewarded by being rudely forced back down.

"Get—get her out of there!" I yelled with a knee in my back. "The bathroom. Door—is locked. Won't budge. Couldn't get her out. Tried. Lord, I tried."

"Who, sir? Who is in the bathroom?" one of them asked, suddenly focusing his firearm somewhere else.

"My wife. My wife—and my baby," I gasped. "Please. Get them out."

I watched the officer cautiously move toward the bathroom door, prepared for possible threats, as he was trained. When he grasped the knob, it turned freely in his grasp. The door gently gave way, opening as if never a barrier.

Within seconds of entering, he yelled out, "All clear! If somebody was in here, they're not anymore."

"Huh? No—" I gasped.

"Sir, there's no one in there," the one standing over me chided, sounding miffed. "And you're under arrest. You have the right to remain silent . . ."

Last words I heard as all went black, finally succumbing to my injuries.

41

I woke up in the hospital; just prior to surgery. Tried to make me understand the reason for drilling a hole in my head and inserting a catheter. Sounded like the teacher from Charlie Brown.

Said I needed decompression and something drained. Maybe they just needed to suck out all the ignorance and stupidity in which I'd been engaging. If that was the case, go ahead and drill a few more holes.

The hovering heads in scrubs kept telling me everything was going to be okay. And because they smiled, that was supposed to make it so.

But they didn't know.

Couldn't know.

Life wasn't filled with simple, pat answers.

Sometimes you have to fight for answers. And sometimes the answers are more than you can handle.

When I woke up, I was screaming for Ava and our child; demanding that they be found. No one knew who or what I was talking about. Told me I'd sustained a traumatic subdural hematoma when the taxi hit me; a slow bleeder as one doctor quipped. Blamed my not making sense on it and assured me all would be better after the emergency surgery. And then they'd remove the restraints on the side of the bed.

Backwards from ten, I counted.

Ten, nine, eigh—

I regained consciousness in a private room. My mom was there.

Steadfast. Resolute. Happy.

I smiled at her, realizing how lucky I was. Still weak as a kitten, but free of the excruciating pain.

"Chase!" she howled when she saw the recognition in my eyes. I went to give her a hug, but couldn't. Cushioned straps still kept me restrained. Somehow they'd rigged one to accommodate my cast.

And a police officer stood in the hallway just outside my door. The uniformed man stared at me through the small crack in the door, then reached for his radio.

"I got my own bodyguard?"

My mother shook her head. "No, boy. They tryin' to charge you. I told them you need your rest and that you got a lawyer, so don't even come around here with that mess."

"Charge me with what? What did I do?" I asked, suddenly trying to recall the many things I'd done. Had Jacobi sold me out with the break-in? That wouldn't be much of a stretch for that snake.

"That art woman went missin'," my mom answered, her voice going lower as her gaze locked on me. "Somebody thinks they saw you at her place."

"Oh," I said, looking away. Wondered how jacked up my head looked from the surgery. I wanted to share all I'd experienced that night with her. Things that challenged the imagination. And science. Things I probably never would comprehend. The only certainty was that Ava was gone. Probably never to return. I just hoped and prayed that wherever she went with our child, that her home was a better world than this one. That damn place with the funny sailboats. I laughed, hurting my head.

"That's all you got to say? Why you laughin'? Please tell me you—"

"They're okay, Mom. I mean it."

"Who's *they*?"

"I meant *she*. Still groggy from . . . everything." She was going to be a grandmother and would never see her grandbaby. Couldn't explain it to her anyway.

"If she's okay, why don't you tell them where she's at?" she asked, motioning toward the room door. "Then they can quit hanging around like damn vultures."

"Because I can't say, Mom. Let's leave it at that."

My mom looked to challenge me. Went to say something, then thought better of it.

"How is Dawn? And Dad?"

"They both better now that you've been found."

"Dawn . . . She's been around?"

"She calls. She calls," my mom answered by not answering. Wouldn't blame her if she moved on.

"Next time she calls, tell her I'm sorry."

There was a quick staccato rap on the room door, followed by a doctor entering who had no plan on waiting for an invite. My mom and I came to attention.

"Good afternoon, Mr. Hidalgo. Ma'am," the WASP-ish physician offered in a distinct fast clip. Probably moved to Texas from somewhere on the East Coast where everything was more hurried and more expensive. He came bedside, excusing himself as he squeezed by my mom. Checked the dressing on my head while grunting to himself in approval of his handiwork.

"Would you like for me to speak to you alone?"

"Nah. My mom is good," I teased. "But you can undo these straps."

"Sorry. Just a precaution. You have been a little unruly. But I'll talk to somebody," he said, cheesing like I was a little kid who he'd just promised ice cream if they behaved. I knew HPD had as much to do with this as the hospital. He glanced at his chart again after running a penlight in front of my eyes. "We ran another CT scan when the ambulance brought you in. Compared it to the one taken at Ben Taub. You were definitely in worse shape. What made you run out of a good trauma center like that? The food?" he joked.

"Like you said, my mind wasn't right."

"All that Motrin you were taking didn't help. Quite the opposite. Probably exacerbated the situation with your subdural hematoma. You thought you were treating the pain, but you were adding a blood thinner to the mix. Yep. Increased the bleeding up in the old noggin," the doctor said, feeling demonstrative. "And you were right about not being 'right.' Um . . . let's see. Irritability? Pain? Headaches? Disorientation? Nausea? Personality changes? Difficulty walking? Blurred vision? Any of that sound familiar?"

I nodded, but Earnestine nodded more. Of course they tried to attribute all my symptoms to the spill I'd taken combined with my earlier car wreck. My mom was overly eager to accept that. Because it meant her son wasn't crazy.

"There is something that stumped us, though," he added, turning to detective mode. "Radiation."

"You mean like from X-rays?"

"No. This is different. In addition to the hematoma, you show exposure to radiation, Mr. Hidalgo. Cosmic rays. Really odd. Just trace amounts now, but . . . Been anywhere unusual lately? Like up in space?"

I began laughing. "Cosmic rays? You mean like the *Fantastic Four*? I used to read their comic book when I was a kid. Am I going to burst into flames? Or begin stretching? I better not turn all rocky, like the Thing."

Doc said nothing. Didn't appreciate being ridiculed. I thought back to my nosebleeds and some of the other symptoms the night I chased Ava. The night the lights came for her. And our baby. I suddenly reflected on the unusual phrases Ava used and that book on parallel universes on her nightstand that I saw once. Doc would get nothing out of me. "Maybe you'll just turn invisible. Like Sue Storm," he finally replied.

"Touché, doc," I responded, appreciating his comic book knowledge.

"Glad I was able to lift your spirits. I'll be in later to harass you again."

Pulling on my restraints, I answered smartly, "I'll be waiting."

"Hmph. They coulda undid those cuffs. Got you shackled like some kind of runaway slave. All that and the doctor said you weren't in your right mind," my mom rattled off as soon as the doctor had cleared out.

"I think the cuffs issue is about to be resolved, Mom," I replied, spying the gentleman speaking with the police officer outside the room door. He didn't waste any time coming in once he saw the doctor had left.

"Mr. Hidalgo. I'm Detective Melendez with HPD. I apologize if this is a bad time. . . ."

Would there ever be a good time?

I remained silent as I watched the detective's mouth run. After all that had occurred, it was now time to face the music.

42

I'd come to know Detective Melendez pretty well since the day he read me my rights at the hospital: An aggressive, hard-nosed cop who liked to sink his teeth into a case and not let go. Mysteries were his enemy. In that case, I'm sure I was frustrating to him.

Or rather my attorney was.

"C'mon, we got the medical records on his person! Records stolen from Dr. Prisbani's office the night before this lady disappeared. Right after your client fled Ben Taub Hospital! Don't deny it!"

"From what I understand, those records were present in the house on Nicholson, but weren't in his possession."

"So who else put them there? The tooth fairy? Jeezuz! He was there alone!" he growled as he abruptly left his seat across the tiny table from us and paced the room. When he returned, he leaned across the table without sitting. Looked at me briefly, then spoke to my lawyer. "At a minimum, we've got your client on breaking and entering."

"We might be willing to concede that point, Detective. But need I remind you that my client was suffering from a subdural hematoma and wasn't in full possession of his faculties."

"Yeah, yeah. I know. I was at the hospital. His brain had an *owie*. I heard that bullshit," he obliged with a little bit of salty language. "But I think we can make

a case. Your client's life is in disarray. At least two as-
saults that witnesses can confirm, even if no charges were
filed. There are reports of an argument between Ms.
Nuttier and him at the art gallery. And now your client's
wife has filed for divorce. I can connect the dots, Counselor."

I tried to conceal my surprise, but was unable to re-
strain a noticeable flinch. My lawyer, sensing the news
unsettled me, just like the detective wanted, patted me
on the leg. Dawn was serious about moving on.

"What do you want from me?" I asked, disobeying the
instructions of my lawyer . . . Maryann Milner. My former employer.

"What I want to know is, What did you do to Charla
Nuttier? Is that why you broke into the house on Nicholson? To hide out? Guilt? Where is her body!"

"Stop right there, Detective!" Maryann shouted. "My
client has obliged your fantasies, but you and I both know
you have no evidence of this. In fact, to the contrary, I
have affidavits from the cabdriver who stated my client
was distraught that night and looking for Ms. Nuttier
out of concern. He certainly didn't want her killed. Besides, we now know that Charla Nuttier isn't even her
real name. Perhaps she had some secrets to hide. Or reason to disappear. Oh. And there's this."

Maryann removed a single document from her briefcase and slid it toward the detective. I tried reading it
upside down, but the detective scooped it up and digest-
ed its nature. Watched him stew for a moment before
speaking.

"Who the hell is Smith Sampson?" Detective Melendez
growled. One of the other people in the room who'd remained silent in the corner during our powwow came
over. The brother in a top-end store-bought suit read
over the document as well then whispered something

in Detective Melendez's ear. Then the two of them hastily left the room.

"What's going on?"

"Your get-out-of-jail-free card, Chase," Maryann said, the barest hint of a smile showing.

"Now just keep your mouth shut."

Outside the room, something was going on. A heated argument between Detective Melendez and someone else, by the sound of the voices. Then all fell silent.

Detective Melendez returned. Didn't bother sitting down and didn't bother to look at Maryann as he addressed her. Kept his eyes on me.

"Will that be all?" she asked.

"You've posted bail. You can go. But don't leave town. We'll let you know if we have further questions."

"I'm sure you will, Detective," Maryann chimed as she pulled her chair away from the table and motioned for me to follow her. She left her business card behind on the table, presumably to further frustrate Detective Melendez.

"Thank you," I told Maryann as we exited HPD headquarters and stepped into the fresh air on Travis Street. I wanted to give her a hug, but it didn't seem appropriate, based on her demeanor.

"Just doing my job . . . my feelings for you aside."

"I didn't do anything to her. I promise."

"I know. I've been assured of that. Still doesn't stop you from being a cheating spouse."

"True, and I'm going to do my best to repair that damage. Heal those wounds with Dawn even if she doesn't take me back. By the way, I never slept with our client Iris."

"Didn't think so, Chase. But what's done is done. The firm could never take you back after all this negative attention. For what it's worth, your former friend Jacobi will never make partner as long as I have a say."

"So who hired you? I know it wasn't Jacobi. And what was that document you gave the detective?"

"I'll let Smith discuss that with you," Maryann replied, signaling with her eyes to look across the street. I complied to see Smith Sampson in a blue T-shirt and white old-man shorts standing around. With his sweatband he had a serious eighties vibe going on. From the sweat-soaked shirt, it appeared he'd been jogging. He waved at us like he didn't have a care in the world.

"Friend of yours?" I asked, suddenly figuring who could afford Maryann's retainer.

"We go back a ways," she replied, finally cracking a smile. "I've known Smith since he first came here from New York. Ran into him in Katz's Deli and we hit it off. Helped introduce him to the gay and lesbian community around town and he's just taken off. Well, I'm sure you two have much to discuss. Go talk to him. I have a lunch fund-raiser to attend. Be well, Chase."

I thanked Maryann a final time, leaving her to follow her schedule. I crossed the street over to Smith, who was jogging in place while looking at his watch.

"Hello, Mr. Hidalgo," he said. "Care to take a walk?"

"Sorry about slapping you back at the art gallery," I said, trying clumsily to break the ice.

"Apology accepted. I like my slaps a little less rough from my men. And never to the face," Smith said, displaying a bit of crude humor as we walked along. Awkward silence followed once more.

"Should I be thanking you for the bail and the lawyer?"

"I suppose. Ava would've wanted it," he said as we came to McKinney and made a right turn.

"What was that paper Maryann gave the police?"

"An affidavit I signed. Attesting that Ava told me she was leaving the country. No evidence of a crime and no evidence of Charla Nuttier being who she really is, no case. Poof."

"And they're not going to push to find out who she really is?"

"Chase, look around. Houston is classified as a sanctuary city to the undocumented," he offered with a grin. "What's one more even if from another world?"

"Do you believe that? That she went home?" I asked of the only other person who might not think me crazy.

"I do," Smith said with a nod and conviction in his eyes. "And who's to say there aren't others out there?"

"Wait," I said, stopping in my tracks. "*Are you one?*"

"From her Earth?" he said coyly. "No, dear man. I wish. Seems like a nice place, until her husband died."

"But when you say others—"

"Why would there be just one parallel world? Say there are others and that, from time to time, people pop through for whatever reasons—fate, second chances, lost loves. Maybe vibrational frequencies line up or perhaps it's simple random chance. Maybe some come from places far worse than this. Maybe someone popped through perhaps a long time ago. Say, like Manhattan in the 1970s."

"You?" I asked, stunned. "Could you go back one day? Like Ava?"

"If—if it were me, I couldn't ever go back. That location no longer exists on this side. Unless I took a helicopter ride over restricted space or can suddenly fly. Haven't quite mastered that one yet," he said with a hearty laugh.

"Huh?"

"The World Trade Center. The forty-third floor of the south tower. That may be where someone like myself came through. But it's no longer there."

"Oh my God."

"Breathe. It'll be okay, Mr. Hidalgo. Some feel the pull to return more strongly than others . . . can't resist. I never had that problem. Thank God. Perhaps that's why I was left here—to help others like Ava."

"Does Maryann Milner know the truth about you?"

"No. And neither did Ava. She just looked at me as a good friend. The less the better. As you can see, things can get awfully difficult when people bring up such things. They instantly think you're crazy or unstable."

"Is Smith Sampson even your real name?"

"Of course it is. Now," he added with a grin. "But like I said, I've been here a while."

"Do you miss home?"

"No. I'm much happier here. Mine is far different than dear Ava's. People like me were persecuted there," he remarked, a less whimsical tone intruding for the briefest of moments. "Like I said. Maybe it's fate when people pop over. Ava got to see you again . . . so to speak."

"You know she's pregnant."

"Yes. She told me. Interesting," Smith said, assessing something in his head. "Maybe that's what triggered her return. Perhaps her purpose here was fulfilled. Just know the baby's in a good place and that they'll want for nothing. Ava's a millionaire over there. And the baby will grow up knowing his or her parents loved one another despite your *confusion*."

"Her. It's a girl," I uttered on reflex, stopping dead in my tracks.

"How . . . how do you know?"

"Dunno," I replied, expressionless. "Can't explain it. Just a hunch that overcame me."

"Hmm," Smith mumbled as he stared oddly at me for a brief moment. "These crossover unions are always intriguing."

"Think I'll see them again?"

"Who's to say? She loves you, Chase. Just take that and run with it. Learn from it. Grow. Oh," he said, checking his watch. "Speaking of 'run,' time's up. Thanks for being my therapist."

With that, the odd old dude with the sweatband jogged away, resuming his pace down McKinney toward Discovery Green Park.

A visitor more comfortable with himself and this world than I.

Recently—Somewhere on I-10 in Louisiana

A bad storm front rolling in from Texas had rendered visibility almost down to zero. A flock of illuminated brake lights had guided me this far. I'd come over the big bridge past the ubiquitous chemical plants and the town of Westlake, crossing the body of water from which the city of Lake Charles got its name, relying on my GPS. Checking the clock in the car, I had time to spare.

I still held on to the microcassette from Dr. Prisbani's file on Ava.

All this time.

Had avoided it until now, but had begun listening to some of Ava's session on the drive in. Appropriate at this moment, I guess. Finally off probation for breaking and entering and no threat of further charges called for a trip such as this. Decided to pull into North Beach, just off I-10 and wait out the weather.

While watching whitecaps atop the gray water and staring at the Lake Charles Civic Center along the shore just southeast of me, I pushed *play* again. Going back in time several years to when I was happily married and hadn't met Ava.

Yet.

"What are you thinking about now?" Dr. Prisbani asked of Ava.

"Chase," she answered. Was odd. Hearing my name, but someone else being referenced. Missed the sound of her voice, though.

"What about him?"

"Remember how I was crying over him in the bathroom when I came here."

"When you say *here*, you're still referring to coming to this world from someplace else?" From her notes, I knew how skeptical Dr. Prisbani was about Ava's claims.

"Yes, that's it. Was thinking of happier times. Thinking back to how he would sneak away after we made love. He'd think I was asleep, but sometimes I would get up and follow him."

"And? What was he doing?"

"He'd be all alone. In the dark . . . just playing the piano in our front room. It was the most beautiful thing to just listen to the music pouring from his soul. Like to think that maybe he was inspired. I hold on to that."

"That is a positive, Ava. Is there something you wish you could take back or do over?"

"Yes. We had an argument before he left for his trip."

"About?"

"Chase wanted a child. Someone to continue his musical legacy. Like his father. He idolized Joell. Those two had such a strong bond. But I wasn't ready for children. Being selfish I guess. We never argued, but that was a bad one. Don't know how it got out of control. Still don't understand. It was like the wrong things kept being said. Wished I could take it all back. In the end, I told him to go on without me. We slept apart that night and . . . he flew out that morning to . . . the Netherlands to perform. And . . . I never saw him again. He died in a—a—car wreck in Rotterdam."

"Do you need a tissue?" Dr. Prisbani asked of her sniffling subject.

"No. No. I'm okay," Ava replied before she pressed on. "We'd gone to the Netherlands for the first time the year before. It was one of the happiest times in my life.

We promised each other that we'd come back. That trip was supposed to be our return.

"That was my thought when I came here. Happiness . . . and how I'd lost it. Chase was my happiness, Doctor."

I wiped the tears from my eyes, cursing that I'd tortured myself like this. I shut off the recorder and stepped out into the rain. I marched across the clumping beach sand to the water's edge where I hurled both the recorder and microcassette in the lake.

Lightning flashed in the distance. The storm was worsening and wouldn't be any better soon, but I couldn't stop now.

For my journey wasn't over.

Now—Rayne, LA

"Loved one?" he asks, daring to interrupt the moment.

"You might say that," I answer, not taking my eyes off the grave that held a small child.

Rainwater continues to run down my face with a steady stream rolling off my nose.

"I did good, huh?" he asks, proud of his detective skills.

"Yeah, man. And I paid you good."

"*Oui*. You pay good money," he says as he leans over into my space to get a better look at the headstone in the rain. I can smell wet cigar. "And it's her birthday too."

"I noticed."

"Is dat a relative of yours? Your daughter?"

"No," I answer, tired of his presence as I stare at the name chiseled into the marble, nestled in between two little angels: *AVA EVANGELINE FOLSE* "It's my wife."

"Huh? Your *wife*?" he grunts, wiping rain from his face to look at the headstone and tiny grave again. "Whatever. You pay good money," he repeats again.

As he stomps off, I am finally given peace.

"Finally we meet," I mouth.

This was an odd journey. Started with the premise one day that if Ava found me, why couldn't there already be an Ava here.

My Ava claimed she was from Pouppeville, Louisiana. Dr. Prisbani was right in her notes. No such place now. But perhaps in Ava's world it never changed its name to Rayne. It was the longest before I figured to try that angle, but I had the advantage of belief in what my Ava said. Once that domino fell, the rest came into focus.

The person in this grave was taken way too early. Choked on a marble at six years old per the old newspaper article I found in the course of my research. If she'd lived, she would've gone on to attend Sam Houston State University over in Texas.

And I would've met her.

At least, that's my theory.

Don't quite know how these things work.

A light show fills the sky, illuminating a figure that's been standing watching me the whole time. I fall over in the mud in surprise. It comes forward as I pick myself up from the muck.

"What do you want?" the figure demands to know. It's an elderly woman in black. No umbrella. Fair-skinned with silver hair beneath a black church hat that isn't shielding her much from the storm. I look at her a little more closely. The pronounced nose, similar lips, and the familiar texture of her hair that shows. Creole. Then I realize she's not asking me what I want with the cemetery.

But what I want with this grave site.

Hers.

Well . . . not hers directly. Rather, her daughter's.

"You ain't gonna speak?"

"Sorry, ma'am. You startled me."

"Nobody supposed to be here in this rain."

"I was just here paying my respects," I answer.

"You know my family?"

"Uh . . . no, ma'am. Just whenever I see those that departed too early . . . It saddens me."

"Oh," Ava's mom says, softening before my eyes. She really should have an umbrella. "Nobody comes on her birthday anymore except me. It's like people move on."

I walk closer, rain really picking up. Making it harder to talk over nature's din, so I speak up. "I'm sorry to hear that. Maybe I can come out with you next year. Keep you company," I offer.

"Who you?" she asks, a flash of reticence in her hazel eyes.

"Chase, ma'am. Chase Hidalgo," I answer, trying to look proper and respectful while drenched.

"You from around here?" she says. eyeing me. It's as if the rain isn't fazing her. But what's a little harsh weather compared to the loss of a loved one?

"Just passing through. From Texas. But I want to learn more about this town . . . and its people."

"Hmph. You gonna catch pneumonia," she scolds. Reminds me of my mom then. "Do you drink coffee?"

"I do today," I joke.

"I can make you a pot. Tell you more about my lil' Ava. If you want. She was my heart . . . my li'l light. Had big dreams for that one," she says as she shakes her head in regret.

"I'd like to hear about those dreams, ma'am. And about her. I'm sure she was a wonderful daughter," I say to my new friend.

"Hmph. Well, c'mon then. This rain ain't stopping anytime soon. And I don't want you sick."

I take Mrs. Folse's hand and lead her out of Saint's Joseph's Cemetery.

Eager to learn more.

Epilogue

I looked out at the crowd inside the arena as they packed in.

Amazed.

Simply stunned by the gathering of roughly ten thousand folk for the North Sea Jazz Festival.

Specifically at Ahoy Rotterdam in the Netherlands.

Imagine how I felt when the invitation for us came down.

Of course, who wouldn't want to see the newly rejuvenated Joell Hidalgo do his thing. After a year or so of sessions and tutelage from him, I still wasn't that good on piano, but he insisted I accompany him. He was patient. He'd carry me until I was ready to headline one day.

As I was born to do.

While I sat at the piano, adjusting my microphone, I turned and looked at my dad. He smiled at me, doing one of his old signature wiggle moves that meant it was time get this party started. Those that understood yelled in appreciation. If only Earnestine weren't afraid of flying. Besides the amazing people we'd met out here, this sight alone would've been worth it to the spunky little lady from Acres Homes back in Houston, Texas. She'd helped dramatically with Joell's turnaround since a rekindling of something between them I didn't bother questioning.

As far as relationships go, Dawn and I spoke sparingly since our divorce. Told her I was coming out here and she was genuinely happy for me, but I know we'll never be a couple again. Too many secrets, including a child *somewhere*, which I wouldn't dare try to explain. Still, those fractures grow tinier with time. She starts law school in the fall.

My dad blew into his horn, a few warm-up notes as he freestyled in a flurry to a round of cheers from concertgoers from around the world. I grinned as I tickled the ivories in refrain, a pupil in awe of the master.

Was damn proud of Joell. Years of stubbornness and he was finally on his meds faithfully. All these wasted years, I resented him for abandoning me and my mom; for not being there when I needed him.

Turns out . . . he needed me even more.

But enough with the melancholy. Time for the melodies.

"Ahoy Rotterdam!" I belted out to a roar from the throng in attendance. "Thank you for coming out! We've come all the way from America and are thrilled to be here! I'm Chase Hidalgo and we are the new Asylum Seekers! But this is who you came for . . . the man! The legend! The incomparable! World famous! *Joellllllllllllll* Hidalgo!"

I raised my hand to cue the band, counting off, "One, two, three, four—"

Somewhere in this land, a red lighthouse and rocky cliffs were waiting to be discovered once again for the first time. But for now, we were gonna play until they kicked us out the auditorium.

"Who knows what tomorrow holds for you," someone once said to me.

One thing is certain. The possibilities are *endless.*

About the Author

Eric Pete is a national bestselling novelist. His previous works include *Real for Me, Someone's In the Kitchen, Gets No Love, Don't Get It Twisted, Lady Sings the Cruels, Blow Your Mind, Sticks and Stones, Reality Check*, and *Crushed Ice*. He has also contributed to the anthologies *After Hours, Twilight Moods,* and *On the Line*. He currently resides in Texas where he is working on his next novel. His Web site is www.EricPete.com.

Discussion Questions

1. What did you think of the concepts explored in *Piano in the Dark*?

2. Do you think the title *Piano in the Dark* is appropriate for the story? Why?

3. Have you ever met a complete stranger that seemed to know you *too* well or that you clicked with right away?

4. What are your thoughts about Ava? Were you surprised by her story?

5. Why do you feel Chase put up with his workplace situation?

6. Did Jacobi's actions in the end surprise you?

7. Did Smith Sampson and his revelations surprise you?

8. Did you know who was in the grave Chase was visiting before the end of the story?

9. What are your thoughts of Joell Hidalgo and Chase's relationship with him?

Reader Discussion Questions

10. What did you take from this story? What themes resonated with you?

11. What was your favorite scene?

12. Who was your favorite character and why?

13. Would *Piano in the Dark* be a novel you would like to see as a movie? Who would you cast as the characters?

14. Is there another story or novel you feel compares to *Piano in the Dark* either in storyline or vibe?

ORDER FORM
URBAN BOOKS, LLC
78 E. Industry Ct
Deer Park, NY 11729

Name:(please print):_____

Address: _____

City/State: _____

Zip: _____

QTY	TITLES	PRICE
	A Man's Worth	$14.95
	Abundant Rain	$14.95
	Battle Of Jericho	$14.95
	By The Grace Of God	$14.95
	Dance Into Destiny	$14.95
	Divorcing The Devil	$14.95
	Forsaken	$14.95
	Grace And Mercy	$14.95
	Guilty Of Love	$14.95
	His Woman, His Wife, His Widow	$14.95
	Illusions	$14.95
	The LoveChild	$14.95

Shipping and handling - add $3.50 for 1st book, then $1.75 for each additional book.

Please send a check payable to:

Urban Books, LLC

Please allow 4 - 6 weeks for delivery

ORDER FORM
URBAN BOOKS, LLC
78 E. Industry Ct
Deer Park, NY 11729

Name:(please print):_____

Address: _____

City/State: _____

Zip: _____

QTY	TITLES	PRICE

Shipping and handling - add $3.50 for 1st book, then $1.75 for each additional book.

Please send a check payable to:

Urban Books, LLC

Please allow 4 - 6 weeks for delivery